SOULWORM

Edward Willett

Royal Fireworks Press

Unionville, New York

Toronto, Ontario

Royal Fireworks Press
First Avenue, PO Box 399
Unionville, NY 10988-0399
(914) 726-4444
FAX: (914) 726-3824
email: rfpress@ny.frontiercomm.net

Royal Fireworks Press
78 Biddeford Avenue
Downsview, Ontario
M3H 1K4 Canada
FAX: (416) 633-3010

ISBN: 0-88092-411-X

Printed in the United States of America using vegetable-based inks on acid-free recycled paper by the Royal Fireworks Printing Co. of Unionville, New York.

1

The New Acolyte

The lights of the car slashed through the deluge, twin spears of illumination impaling falling raindrops that glittered silver against the blackness of the wet pavement, the wet sky, the wet world.

The engine screamed as the driver's right foot pressed harder. A green number flickered on the dash, jumped upward by twos and threes. The boy at the wheel laughed. The girl snuggled close at his right laughed with him. The girl in the back seat did not. Mouth dry, she clung to the upholstery. The scornful eyes of the boy mocked her in the rearview mirror. "Having fun?" he yelled, jerking the wheel from side to side. Tires squealed and the car lurched drunkenly.

But then he must have seen the terror on the backseat passenger's face, for his eyes flicked back to the road ahead—or where the road should have been.

Still accelerating, the car shot off the curve and arced through the air. Its nose dropped lazily, smashed through a barbed-wire fence, then plowed into the muddy summerfallow field beyond. The car flipped onto its back, skidded sideways in the mire, and rolled six times in a welter of mud and water, tortured metal and breaking glass, leaving a trail of torn earth and scattered bits of chrome and steel.

It ended on its back, in a growing puddle of oil and gasoline. A pickup truck squealed to a stop on the curve just as the wreck burst into flames, burning eagerly despite the rain.

As the horrified driver of the pickup leaped out, he saw in the lurid light two figures on opposite sides of the wreck, one lying deathly still, the other sitting in the mud, slowly rocking back and forth.

All too clearly, he also saw a third figure, trapped in the driver's seat, enveloped in fire.

      ♌   ♌   ♌   ♌   ♌

Fire, leaping and crackling, encircled the two old women like a wall. Flames and heat-shivered air obscured them, but Liothel, though at the very back of the crowd of Acolytes, could plainly discern the exorcism's progress.

I ought to be able to, she thought. *I've watched enough of them.*

The old woman on the right, brought bound to Wardfast Mykia only that morning, began to sway, her face screwed tight in pain or concentration. Her hands, tied together with scarlet rope, clenched and unclenched spasmodically, and Liothel, seeing that, knew the climax was near.

The Exorcist, a taller woman wearing the blue robe of a Warder, stood statue-still, face calm, eyes closed. Not all Exorcists were so composed as they went about their task, Liothel knew; but then, Yvandel was Mykia's Exorcist Mother. She was supposed to be the best.

Just in front of Liothel a gaggle of Acolytes squirmed and elbowed and whispered. "I can't see—can you see?" "I can't see either." "What's going on?" "Is it over yet?" "Where's the soulworm?"

Liothel resisted the impulse to swat them from behind. It wasn't her place; though she was years older, she, too, was only an Acolyte—and they knew it very well, and would be only too happy to remind her, probably for several days, if she overstepped her authority. For a moment even her clear view of the proceedings galled her; the only reason she could see so well was that she stood a full head taller than any of the others. Her gray Acolyte's robe had had to be specially made for her. She should already be a Warder....

The empty eyes of Blind Maris, the Wardfast Sentinel, who stood at her post by the courtyard gate only a few feet away, swung toward Liothel, who hastily touched forehead, mouth and chest in the Warders' Sign. Such resentful thoughts were dangerous this near an about-to-be-exorcised soulworm, no matter how brightly the Circle of Fire burned!

And it burned very bright indeed, as Second Warrior Teressa added more fuel to the flaming trench surrounding Yvandel and the soulworm-possessed. Like Liothel, Teressa knew the exorcism was almost complete—

Suddenly the possessed woman stiffened, then collapsed; but her shadow remained standing.

The fidgety young Acolytes quieted, staring; Liothel shivered, even though she had seen it so many times. A thin, wavering cry seemed to echo around the courtyard, though Liothel knew the sound was only in their minds. Yvandel remained unmoving and unmoved.

The shadow-shape spun in place, losing form, dwindling. It darted at Yvandel, but could not touch her; reached out for its former host, and found her likewise unassailable. And all the while the flames leaped around it, their light burning it away, evaporating it, driving it into...

...nothingness.

The shadow was gone. The flames sank. And Yvandel knelt beside the other woman, who opened her eyes...and smiled.

A sigh ran around the courtyard, a sigh interrupted by the deep voice of Guardian Mother Amaryl, who had watched all from an overlooking balcony. "One hour of meditation. Then meet with your tutors to discuss what you have seen." She tapped her white staff of office three times. "I declare this gathering of the Warders of Mykia ended."

The Acolytes scattered in twos and threes, voices rising in excited chatter. Liothel, alone as usual, was stopped at the gate by Blind Maris. "No meditation for you, young lady," said the old woman. She reached out with uncanny accuracy and took the sleeve of Liothel's robe. "I'll not have you brooding. You come with me—there's a bit of work you can help me with. Avondia?"

"Here, mistress." A young Warder, the same age as Liothel, appeared on the other side of the gate.

"I think we've kept that new applicant waiting long enough. While we Test her, this lass," she nodded toward Liothel, "will serve as recorder. She needs to think of something besides how put-upon she is."

"I wasn't—" Liothel began.

"I Read you," Blind Maris said. "You were."

Liothel swallowed her protest, and followed the Sentinel and her apprentice down the twisting, narrow lane between high stone walls that led from the Courtyard of Exorcism to the Gatehouse. *What would it be like,* she wondered, *to be able to reach into other people's minds and sense their thoughts?* There could be no secrets from the Sentinel.

Maybe it's no wonder she lives in the Gatehouse, as far as possible from the Keep, Liothel thought, and felt a little ashamed for thinking—and a lot more ashamed when Avondia glanced back at her, for Avondia, of course, shared her mistress's gift.

Liothel dropped back a little more, though only the Creator knew how far was far enough to keep Maris or even Avondia from reading her mind. She and Avondia used to be friends, when they were both Acolytes—before Avondia's latent Talent had manifested itself two years before, and she had become Apprentice Sentinel. Now she was a Warder, and Liothel—

"Acolyte, please try to keep up," Avondia snapped, and Liothel's mouth tightened. Discord of any kind was fertile ground for the Enemy—but Avondia did not make it easy for Liothel to think kind thoughts.

Avondia led the way through a back entrance to the Gatehouse, down a narrow, dusty corridor, and finally through a barred door into the Chamber of Testing, a large, octagonal room. A gold-embossed eight-pointed star gleamed at the centre of a marble floor hollowed and polished by the nervously shuffling feet of the thousands who had faced Blind Maris or her predecessors there over the centuries.

Liothel sat at the writing desk off to one side, and took out the massive, leather-bound *Book of Records*, a pen and a bottle of ink. Blind Maris, meanwhile, heaved herself into the carved wooden chair that faced the large bronze door in the opposite wall, and nodded to her apprentice.

Avondia opened the door, went out, and returned with a girl a little younger than Liothel; a girl Liothel disliked on sight.

For one thing, she reeked of sweat, fear, blood and smoke—especially smoke. Liothel wrinkled her nose and thought if she were applying to the Warders, she would at least take a dip in the nearest river first. "Clean body, clean soul," said Jara, the Acolytes' chief tutor, when their pre-dinner washing had been just a bit rushed....

But Jara was not there, and Blind Maris, whose nose was sharp as a hound's, seemed not to notice the stench, though Avondia frowned slightly from her place beside the door. Liothel schooled her expression to neutrality and concentrated on recording every word spoken.

"Your name is Kalia," Blind Maris stated, and the applicant's eyes widened at this first taste of the Sentinel's power. "You come to us from Yvol's Hold. A long journey, for one so young. How many summers have you, Kalia of Yvol's Hold?"

"Sixteen," said the girl, her voice strong and confident. *Her short, ragged blonde hair, probably cut with the sheathed knife at her waist, made her look more like a boy a year younger,* Liothel thought. And she had little of a woman's shape to alter that opinion. Though part of that might be due to short rations. Kalia's face was gaunt, as though she had not eaten in days....

"You are hungry, Kalia," said the Sentinel. "Hungry, and cold, too, I'd wager, with the first snow already come and gone and the days dying. Why do you come here, to Wardfast Mykia, instead of going to Wardfast Hethro, which is close by Yvol's Hold?"

"I come here because the war party that pillaged my home rode toward Wardfast Hethro," Kalia snapped, and Liothel's mouth quirked. It did no good to become angry with the Sentinel. It only told her more of what she wanted to know.

"And how much of your desire to be a Warder is really only a wish to be warm and fed?" Blind Maris pressed. "And where will it go when the sun returns and the sap rises? Do you know the oaths we take, lass? One is to be celibate—an oath that means little to most Acolytes, at least at first, but you are years older than our usual applicants, and you are no maiden. I Read that clearly."

"It happened," said Kalia flatly. "There was no child, there was no second time, and I have regretted it since. I am prepared for that sacrifice."

"Hmmm. Well, fear not, young Kalia. Here you will find no young men to tempt you from your rash promise."

The girl's thin, strained face lit up. "You're going to accept me?"

"Indeed."

"But you've only spoken with me for a few minutes—you've asked almost nothing—"

"I have heard what I needed to hear, in your voice, and, more importantly, in your heart. I do not Test you on what you say, child, but on what you don't say. Acolyte Kalia, welcome to Mykia." She embraced the girl, whose eyes shone in the light of the lamps hung beneath the silver dome of the ceiling.

Avondia gave Blind Maris a troubled look, even took half a step forward—then became aware of Liothel's eyes on her and quickly stepped back. Nevertheless, Maris turned her own head slightly, and said warmly to Kalia, "If you'll wait in the anteroom outside for a few minutes, I'll send someone to show you to your quarters and explain how we live here in Wardfast Mykia."

"Yes, my—" Kalia blinked. "Umm, please, ma'am, what do I call you?"

"I am the Sentinel," said Blind Maris. Liothel sensed the extra emphasis she put on that proclamation, and obviously Avondia did, too; her mouth tightened.

"Yes, Sentinel. Thank you. Thank you!" Kalia almost ran from the room.

At once Blind Maris turned to Liothel. "You may cease recording, child." Liothel laid aside her pen and carefully blotted the page before closing the Book.

"Which Warder shall I get to take charge of Kalia, Sentinel?" she asked, thinking she was glad it would not be—

"I think you would be the most appropriate choice," said Blind Maris.

Liothel stared. "I? But, Sentinel, I'm only an Acolyte—"

"And were feeling sorry for yourself in that regard only moments ago, were you not? Liothel, there are tasks other than the use of the Talents that are also important to the Wardfast. You have a latent Talent, as does that girl I just Tested, or you would not be an Acolyte. Just because it is late manifesting does not make you any less vital to Mykia. Perhaps this small task will help you understand that. Besides, you have lived here since you were a baby and are most familiar with our ways. Who better to welcome Kalia? Particularly since she is closer to your age than to the other Acolytes."

"But, Sentinel—"

"And also, Liothel," said Blind Maris inexorably, turning her blank, but somehow penetrating, gaze on her, "I Read your unkind feelings toward this girl who has come to us homeless and frightened, bereft of all family and friends. She is alone in this world. She needs our compassion. You need to learn to give it."

Liothel felt ashamed. She had been unkind and unfair toward Kalia, about whom she knew almost nothing. It bothered her—she had never thought herself one to make snap judgments about people.

"I think it is because Kalia is so near your own age that you have these unworthy feelings," said the Sentinel, again uncannily picking up on her thoughts. "You have always been either younger or older than the other Acolytes. Deep in your heart you fear Kalia could somehow be your competitor, could take your place in our affections. Search your feelings and see if this is not so—and overcome it. It will strengthen you as a Warder."

8

Liothel made the Warder's Sign, knowing Maris would sense it, even though she could not see. "Your wisdom, as always, enriches me."

"My wisdom, I fear, is not something universally agreed upon," Maris said drily, inclining her head toward Avondia, who frowned and looked down. "Go to Kalia, child. Make her welcome."

"Yes, Sentinel." Liothel crossed the eight-pointed star to the door.

As Avondia strode past her in the opposite direction, Liothel heard Maris's patient sigh. "So, Apprentice, tell me what it is you sense that you think I have not."

"It was only a tinge of darkness on the fifth level, Sentinel, but I swear..."

Liothel went through the bronze door, and its closing cut off the increasingly technical exchange. For a moment she stood there, waiting for her eyes to adjust to the much dimmer light of the single oil lamp that lit the short hall to the antechamber, and thought about what Maris had said. Could she actually be jealous of someone she had never met until now, a boyish girl with ragged hair and dirty clothes stinking of battle?

"No!" her surface mind proclaimed fiercely...but "yes," whispered a quieter voice within, and there she found the truth. Yes, she could be jealous, jealous of a girl who at least had known her parents, had known friends and laughter and the normal life of a village instead of the daily sameness of life in the Wardfast, had even known the touch of a man...all things she had never known, would never know; things that had been taken from her when, as an infant, she had been left at the gate of Wardfast Mykia, and the Sentinel had sensed, even then, in her unformed mind, her potential Talent.

She shook her head. So, she was jealous. Facing that unpleasant truth, she could move beyond it. She had to move beyond it, to become a Warder when (if, whispered a voice from even further within) her Talent manifested. There could be no hidden envies, no masked rivalries, among the Warders. Such emotions were the food of the soulworms, the Enemy.

But as she strode down the hallway and stepped through a blue-curtained archway into the antechamber, and saw and smelled Kalia again, she realized simply facing her emotions was not the same as banishing them, for the instant dislike she had felt on first seeing the other girl rose in her once more.

"Kalia," she said, in as warm a tone as she could manage. "My name is Liothel. I am also an Acolyte. I welcome you to Mykia."

"I saw you—in the other room." Kalia stood up from the embroidered green-velvet couch that was the antechamber's principal furnishing and smiled tentatively. "You were writing down everything that was said, weren't you?"

"The words of every Testing are written in the *Book of Records*. The deeper Testing, the Sentinel writes in her heart."

"I really didn't understand that," said Kalia. "What was she testing for?"

Liothel opened her mouth to reply, but was cut off by Avondia, who emerged through the curtain, thrusting it aside almost angrily. "We Test for potential Talent—and for possession by the Enemy."

Kalia's eyes widened. "Soulworms?"

"Those of us with the talent of Testing can sense them lurking inside a mind—and the Sentinel is the greatest Tester in the Wardfast." Her eyes never left Kalia's face.

10

"Soulworms," Kalia repeated slowly. "Of course. You had to know if I were demon-possessed—"

"They're not demons," Liothel broke in, disturbed by Avondia's strange manner and even more by the absence of Blind Maris. Avondia was never to leave her mistress's side—never! Liothel was no Sentinel, but even she knew that. "That's what the superstitious call them. Warders know better. There's no doubt they are evil, but they aren't supernatural in any way. They're created beings, like you and me, or hounds and horses. They live to eat and to reproduce. Unfortunately—"

"Unfortunately," Avondia said softly, "they thrive on the negative emotions—anger, lust, and hate. They infiltrate their victims, influence their actions, stimulate these emotions in their host and others around them, and feed, and grow; and when the time is right, in a paroxysm of physical violence, they spawn, and a single soulworm becomes nine, or ten, or a dozen or more, and the cycle repeats." She suddenly stepped forward and touched Kalia's forehead. The girl jerked away, startled, and Avondia stood as if transfixed for a moment before lowering her hand. "It is our greatest dread," she whispered, "that one day a soulworm will infiltrate a Wardfast." And with that she strode past them, through the door to the rest of the Gatehouse.

Kalia stared after her. "What was that all about?"

"I don't know." Liothel glanced back at the curtained arch leading to the Chamber of Testing, then became aware of Kalia's curious gaze, cleared her throat and turned around. "I think it's time I showed you around," she said, crossing to the door. "Starting with the baths!"

2

Wardfast Mykia

The young man from the pickup ran across the field, the mud sucking at his feet as though trying to hold him back from the horror ahead. He could no longer even tell if the driver had been male or female; he turned away, stomach churning. The supine figure closest to him proved to be a girl about sixteen, and he saw at once that her leg was broken. Blood covered her clothes. The flames from the wreckage flickered in her open eyes. "Are you all right?" he asked inanely, but she didn't move, didn't make a sound, didn't so much as blink.

On the other side of the wreckage a girl about the same age sat with her arms wrapped around her legs, rocking back and forth, crying; but she didn't respond either when he spoke to her, and when he pulled her up and tried to get her to walk to the pickup she sat right back down again in the mud.

Finally, desperate, he left her and ran back across the field, staggering through the clinging muck. He had to get help.

ꘜ   ꘜ   ꘜ   ꘜ   ꘜ

The easiest path to the baths would have been around the wall that encircled the hill Mykia crowned, but the more strenuous route, over the hill's crest, would allow Liothel to show Kalia more of the Wardfast. So she led the new Acolyte out of the rambling, gray-stone Gatehouse and into the light of the late-autumn sun, already dropping toward the western wall. Kalia looked around eagerly. "It's just like a village!"

"Like yours?" Liothel asked, then bit her lip; Kalia's village no longer existed.

But Kalia didn't seem to mind. "No, much larger. And so much stone and so little wood..."

"Fire is an important part of some of our rituals," Liothel said. "Now, up these steps—the baths are on the far side of the hill, and between here and there you'll see all there is to see of Wardfast Mykia."

As they walked she tried very hard to put her unreasoning dislike of Kalia behind her. How could she not like a girl who showed such pleasure in the simplest things—the smith, the tailor, the grooms exercising the Wardfast's precious horses—even though she must have seen them all her life in her own village? Her interest made Liothel take a second look at these familiar people, too, who nodded to her politely as she passed. All of them were women, of course; men were not allowed within the walls of Mykia. Some of them came from nearby villages and farms; others were women who had come to Mykia for refuge, usually from husbands who beat them or other trouble at home, and still others were failed applicants, who had been sent to Mykia by their families as young girls but had been found to have no Talent. Many such returned home, but some were not welcome to return, and so they remained, and found a place in the Wardfast even though they could never contribute directly to Mykia's most important work, the continuing battle against the soulworms. Kalia smiled at them all, but Liothel could not; as every day passed without her Talent manifesting, she feared that she, too, would end up here, currying horses or washing clothes, the only Acolyte to be accepted and then to fail.

She was glad when their steps took them up from the lower reaches to the inner walls, the walls that shut off the spiritual heart of the Wardfast from the necessary noise and bustle of its physical maintenance. The gates swung open at their approach and closed behind them at the behest of hidden guards, and they entered a garden touched by frost, but still beautiful.

Protected from the wind, yellow leaves shimmered on silver-gray trees, and the path of crushed white stone that wound through the brown grass glowed like snow in the light of the lowering sun. "Imagine it in spring," Liothel said wistfully. "It's my favorite place."

"It's lovely," said Kalia, and Liothel gave her a sharp look, thinking she heard sarcasm. But Kalia's face was alive with interest, her bright eyes darting everywhere, as though trying to see everything at once.

"On our way back, we'll climb up there." Liothel pointed across the garden to the soaring central tower of the tall, many-turreted Keep. "From there, you can see the whole Wardfast."

"Why not now?"

"See that banner?" A silver streamer floated from the tower's top. "That means the Inner Circle is meeting and the tower is locked and guarded. But they'll be done before we can get back. And we have to come back this way anyway. That's where the Acolytes and Warders all live."

"In that tower?"

Stupid, Liothel thought, then caught Kalia's smile and realized it was a joke. She forced a smile in return. "It would be a tight fit. I meant the whole building—the Keep, we call it. A place of peace. The center of our lives." She led Kalia around it, pointing out the windows of Acolyte's Hall, three stories up on the east side, then took her out through the far gate of the inner wall, and down through the trees and rocks that covered that steeper side of the hill to the bathhouse. Liothel smiled at the thought of the hot water promised by the smoke rising from the bathhouse's tall chimney. Kalia might be the one who really needed a bath, but she could use a relaxing soak herself. She felt like a viol string being tuned higher and higher the longer she was with Kalia. *We must make her welcome,* she told herself for the tenth or eleventh time. *You must make her welcome. She is your sister now....*

It was still early in the day for baths; the big pool was tranquil and empty. Liothel showed Kalia where she could put her clothes to have them washed, but added, as she stripped off her own long gray robe and then her short white chemise, "You won't need those anymore, anyway. We can get you clean Acolyte's garments here, and those will be sent to our room later."

"You can burn them for all I care," said Kalia, disrobing at once and tossing her clothes in the cloth bag Liothel indicated. Her thin body was covered with bruises, welts and scabs, and Liothel felt guilty again for her unkind thoughts. But she couldn't seem to help them. She took a bone marker with her initial on it from a rack on the wall and slipped it into the bag with the clothes, then dashed for the pool.

To her surprise, Kalia passed her like the wind and dove in so smoothly she raised hardly a splash, and Liothel felt yet another pang of jealousy as she made her own noisy entry.

But some of her aversion to Kalia eased as they splashed and laughed together, then moved to the soaping pool and lathered each other's hair. When at last they emerged from the bathhouse, clean and dry (though it seemed to Liothel a faint smell of smoke still hung around the other girl), Liothel was able to meet Kalia's smile and mostly mean it.

15

They climbed companionably back up the hill to the Keep. The Warder at the door welcomed them warmly. "Liothel! Ready for the big day?"

Liothel laughed and said, "This is Kalia, Marthwit, a new Acolyte. She passed her Testing just an hour ago."

"Joyous!" Marthwit gathered Kalia to her ample bosom, and Kalia, whose eyes met Liothel's over Marthwit's shoulder in a mute appeal, returned the hug rather feebly when Liothel only grinned.

"I'd like to take her up the tower," Liothel said. "The banner is down, isn't it?"

"Yes, the Circle broke up twenty minutes ago. But you'd better hurry—you're almost out of sun. And supper's early tonight, to make time for rehearsal afterward."

"Don't worry, we won't be late. Come on, Kalia."

"What was that about a big day? And rehearsal?" Kalia followed Liothel down the long, carpeted hallway, looking from side to side at the rich tapestries depicting the day-to-day life of the Wardfast. Liothel kept her eyes straight forward; though some of the tapestries were centuries old, the scenes they recorded were repeated daily in the Wardfast. The unchanging nature of life in Mykia was not something she enjoyed being reminded of.

"It's only three weeks until Prisca's Day," she answered Kalia.

"What? But..." Kalia's voice trailed off as she apparently did some quick counting in her head. "You're right."

"We do keep track of the anniversary of the founding of the Warders," Liothel said drily. "Through here, and watch your head."

"Through here" was a short, low passageway into a stairwell, and Kalia, being shorter than Liothel by a hand's breadth and then some, did not really have to watch her head, though Liothel bumped hers as she always did. The steps wound around the inner core of the tower, pausing at intervals at landings where torches burned by locked doors. Liothel and Kalia were both breathing hard when at last they emerged onto the top of the tower. *But,* thought Liothel, as she always did at that moment, *it was worth it.*

The sun hung just above the horizon, and its fiery light lit the top branches of the vast forest stretching to the horizon in all directions, though shadow already wreathed the bases of the trees. Here and there cleared fields, long since harvested, glowed like pale jewels in dark green velvet, and whitewashed farmhouse walls turned gold beneath their telltale fingers of smoke.

At the base of the hill wound a river, reflecting the purple sky. It cut close under the outer walls, touching them at the foot of the Gatehouse. A drawbridge spanned the river there, and as Kalia and Liothel stood atop the tower, the cool breeze turning to chill, three riders crossed that bridge, the clatter of their horses' hooves echoing from the water and reaching the tower after the mounted women had already ridden out along the trail into the forest.

"It's beautiful up here," Kalia said, closing her eyes and turning her head to the breeze, her face ruddy in the sun's last rays.

Liothel thought better of her at that moment. "It is," she agreed. "The Keep is a place of peace from door to hearth to window, but up here—up here is special." She grinned. "For one thing, none of the Warders ever climb this far—only Acolytes."

"But didn't you say the—uh, Inner Circle meets up here?"

"In the tower—but not here. They meet behind one of those doors we passed coming up. I don't know which one. No one does. No one except the Inner Circle knows what's

17

behind any of those doors." She stretched luxuriously, closing her eyes and breathing deep, and caught again a whiff of smoke. She wrinkled her nose, wondering where it came from. Surely Kalia couldn't still smell of fire after all that water and soap!

"Where are they going?"

Liothel opened her eyes. "Who?"

"Those riders." Kalia pointed at the trio, passing the nearest farmhouse.

"They're probably the Verification party," Liothel said.

"Verification?"

"Because of your story. They're riding to Yvol's Hold."

Kalia stiffened. "You mean I'm still not trusted? Even after my Testing?"

"What? Of course you're trusted. Maris passed you herself—how could we not trust you?" *How indeed?* she asked herself sternly.

"Then why do they have to verify what I said?"

"That's not what—"

"That's what it looks like to me!"

"Kalia, you reported a violent attack on your village to a Wardfast. The Warders have to see if soulworms were involved. That's why we exist. What did you expect?"

Kalia glared after the vanished party. "It's a long way to Yvol's Hold. And they're wasting their time. There weren't any demons involved—just greedy humans." Her voice was cold.

"Not demons!" Liothel snapped. "Soulworms. If you intend to become a Warder, you'd better forget your superstitions. There's nothing magical about soulworms—I told you that. They're just clever, vicious beasts, that carry violence and bloodshed like rats carry plague. And just because you think they weren't involved doesn't mean a thing. Those men could have been possessed and not even known it. So could you! That's one reason you were Tested. Remember what Avondia said." Avondia. The thought of the strange way the Apprentice Sentinel had acted bothered her. She shivered in a sudden breath of icy air. "Let's go down. It's almost supper time."

She touched Kalia's shoulder, but Kalia jerked away—then turned back at once in apology. "I'm sorry!" She reached out herself and took Liothel's hand. "It's just—I don't like the idea of anyone going to Yvol's Hold. I don't like to think about—that night. What happened."

Liothel could hear the pain in the other girl's voice, and at last compassion woke in her. Kalia might grate on her, for whatever dark reason buried in her own soul, but the girl had lost her parents, her home—and if sometimes Liothel pitied herself for never having had either, how could she not pity someone who had had both, and lost them? Kalia needed a friend. She needed Liothel.

Liothel was not used to thinking of herself as particularly needed by anyone. She squeezed Kalia's hand. "Then don't think about it," she said. "Put it behind you. From now on, we're your family. You're one of us." It was what the Warders told her whenever she let some of her own inner turmoil show. She hoped it made Kalia feel better than it ever had her.

Kalia embraced her, and when she spoke, her voice was muffled by Liothel's shoulder. "You don't know how much that means to me."

Liothel hugged her back, then led the way down the stairs again, past the locked doors hiding the secrets of the Wardfast, down to firelight, friendship and food.

They paused only once, on the last landing, to watch out the narrow window as the sun sank from sight, its red light

19

travelling stone by stone up the walls of the Keep until night covered all of Wardfast Mykia.

3

The Gate

By the time an ambulance, the police and the fire department arrived on the scene, the wreckage had burned out, though it still hissed and popped angrily in the wind-driven rain, now mixed with sleet. The girl with the broken leg no longer stared blankly at the car; she was unconscious. But the other girl still sat rocking in the mud. She allowed herself to be led to the ambulance, but she still didn't speak.

The unconscious girl had more injuries than just the broken leg; a few minutes passed before the ambulance attendants put her on a stretcher and loaded her aboard. As the ambulance turned and raced back toward the city lights on the horizon, one of the four policemen at the scene came over to his partner. "We have names on the two girls," he said. "They were both carrying I.D. The one with the broken leg is named Maribeth Gayle; the other is Christine Redpath. Both sixteen."

"What about the driver?" The other policeman nodded at the sheet-covered body beside the wreckage.

"No way to tell—unless one of the girls starts talking, it may be a while before we know."

"Yeah, this is a real mess, isn't it?"

His partner grimaced. "You can say that again."

♌   ♌   ♌   ♌   ♌

The main entrance to the Great Hall was not far from the door into the tower. Liothel and Kalia slipped in just as Guardian Mother Amaryl rose from her white chair at the Inner Circle's table on the dais at the far end of the hall. Kalia gasped when she saw the vast silver-and-green tapestry that hung behind Amaryl's chair, stretching from the high ceiling's gilded beams to the dark wood of the floor. "It's magnificent!" she breathed.

"Our most prized possession," Liothel whispered as she hurriedly found places for them at one of the long black tables. "It's Prisca, of course." She felt Amaryl's eyes on her, flushed and fell silent.

Amaryl tapped her staff three times, then said, "Peace, sisters." Her voice, neither strident nor loud, nevertheless carried to every corner of the huge hall, and to every one of the more than two hundred Warders gathered there.

"Peace," they replied, the sound like a vast sigh.

"We give special thanks this day for three things. We give thanks that another of the Enemy has been destroyed."

"We give thanks," the Warders repeated.

"We give thanks that Festival approaches."

"We give thanks."

"And we give thanks that we have a new Acolyte. Kalia, will you stand, please?"

Kalia got to her feet, but kept her gaze on the floor.

"We give thanks," the Warders said, most of them turning to look at her.

"And we welcome her to our midst," the Guardian Mother went on.

"Welcome!" everyone said.

Kalia, flushed, sat down again in a hurry.

"Kalia comes to us from Yvol's Hold, and brings the distressing news of that village's destruction by an unidentified war band. Warders Tiella, Sharkan and Esbania have undertaken the Verification. We ask the Creator to guard their safety." She bowed her head in a moment of silent prayer, then raised it and said, "And now, Sisters—eat well!" She banged her staff again and sat down.

At once Acolytes emerged through the swinging doors from the kitchens with steaming tureens of soup and platters of bread and meat, and the roar of conversation rose with the savory smells of the meal.

Liothel expected Kalia to be ravenous, but the new Acolyte only picked at her food, not even answering when the Warder next to her made a friendly comment. Liothel caught the woman's eye and shrugged, and the Warder smiled back and instead engaged in an earnest conversation with the overweight Warder to her left about the relative merits of the various spices in the soup.

"What's wrong, Kalia?" Liothel finally asked, as she soaked a piece of bread in the last of her soup.

"Nothing." Kalia chased a slice of carrot around her plate for a moment, then said, "How long before the Verification Party gets back from Yvol's Hold?"

"I'd guess they'll return around Festival. Why?"

Kalia finally caught the carrot and ate it without enthusiasm. "That's not very long."

"What difference does it make? I thought you didn't like the idea of them going in the first place."

"I didn't...but it occurred to me maybe someone else survived. Since they're going, I wish they'd stay long enough to be sure."

"Don't worry, I'm sure they will." Liothel wiped her mouth with a linen napkin. "Are you finished?"

"Yes." Kalia pushed her still half-filled plate away.

Liothel looked at it. "You're sure?" Kalia nodded. "All right, then, let's go. I'll show you where we sleep."

As they crossed the floor to the Hall entrance, Blind Maris entered, followed, Liothel saw with relief, by Avondia, though the apprentice still wore a frown that grew even sourer when she saw Kalia. "Good evening, Sentinel," Liothel said respectfully. "Apprentice Sentinel."

Maris just nodded, her usually warm expression not much happier than her apprentice's. Avondia said flatly, "Acolytes," gave Kalia a hard look, then followed Maris into the Hall and toward the table of the Inner Circle.

"She doesn't seem to like me," Kalia commented as Liothel led her through corridors and up stairs to the Acolyte's Hall. "How come?"

"I don't know. But don't worry about it. I think her problem is really with Maris. Besides, she doesn't like me much, either." She shook her head. Discord between the Sentinel and her apprentice was not healthy. The Enemy would love it.

Liothel showed Kalia their room, and Kalia undressed and crawled into bed at once, falling asleep almost instantly. Liothel sat up for some time, studying by candlelight for the next day's classes, listening to her new roommate's steady breathing. Once Kalia suddenly rolled over and cried, "Get out!" but she didn't wake, and whatever dream troubled her, it passed as quickly as it had come. As Liothel turned back the covers of her own bed, she looked at the sleeping girl's face, peaceful now in the flickering yellow light, remembered the bruises she had seen on her body, and thought it would have been far more surprising had Kalia not had nightmares.

In the morning, after breakfast in the Hall, Liothel took Kalia to the Acolyte Mother to start her instruction. But the Mother put her off. "Not today, Liothel," she said absently, as she searched for a misplaced tome in the bookshelf that took up one entire wall of her room. "We've got five new Acolytes coming from Swift River in two days—we'll start Kalia with them. Why don't you just take her to your classes? She won't understand much of what you're discussing, but at least she'll get some idea of what life is like here."

"She's right, you know," Liothel warned Kalia as she led her to her first class. "You probably won't get much out of this. I've been studying for years—longer than any other Acolyte—and I still don't understand half of what we talk about."

Kalia shrugged. "I don't mind."

They clattered down a wooden staircase. A cold breath blew over them from an unshuttered window in the stairwell, and Liothel shivered and hurried into the corridor beyond. "You will like the teacher, though: Jara, the chief tutor. I would have introduced you to her yesterday, but she's been at Wardfast Innovar for a month—just got back this morning. She's one of our most powerful Warders; one of only two double-talented Warders in Mykia."

"Double-talented?"

Liothel turned right down a narrower side-corridor. "There are two Gifts, in varying strengths: Detection, sometimes called Testing, and Exorcism. Those with the Gift of Detection can sense the presence of a soulworm. Those whose gifts are particularly strong—like Blind Maris and Avondia—can do even more. They can actually reach inside other people's minds and read their thoughts. That's why Maris is Sentinel. Those with the Gift of Exorcism, like Sharkan, who went to Yvol's Hold for the Verification, are able to drive soulworms out of those they possess. Those with both Gifts are called double-talented—and they're very rare."

"So this Jara can tell, just by looking at someone, if she is possessed, and then drive the soulworm out, just like that?"

"It's not that easy," Liothel said with a laugh. "Unfortunately. It takes a conscious effort—like Maris's in the Chamber of Testing—to detect possession, and it gets harder the longer the soulworm is present in the person. The soulworm learns to cover its traces, to hide itself in the mind of the person it has possessed. And as for Exorcising it—that is even harder, and very draining on the Exorcist. Sometimes they fail. Sometimes, they die. Jara talks of something called 'the battle on the dark plain,' but I'm not really sure what that is."

"What about Warriors? Didn't one of them go to Yvol's Hold, too?"

"That's a purely physical skill. Warriors are usually those with Gifts too low-level to be of much use. They are trained to contain and destroy the soulworm once it is driven out."

"You mean with swords or arrows?"

"No. Though they learn battle skills, too, of course, because of the violence associated with soulworm breeding. But steel is useless against the Enemy. They can only be destroyed by fire. The Warrior builds a ring of fire around the soulworm-possessed, so when it is driven out, it can't escape."

"But can't it fly? I mean, it's not really—"

"I keep telling you: soulworms are creatures, not ghosts or demons. They can no more fly than you can."

For a few minutes they walked in silence, but as they rounded the last corner before reaching Jara's room, Kalia asked, "And what Gift do you have?"

Liothel stopped with her hand on the latch, feeling her face go hot, but bit back a sharp reply. Kalia couldn't know how that question hurt her. "I haven't manifested any Gift," she said levelly. "That's why I'm still an Acolyte." Then she opened the door.

Jara was already there, and when she turned and saw Liothel her lined face creased in a smile that seemed to set lamps alight in her blue eyes. "Liothel!"

Liothel felt her own heart lifting again, as it always did in Jara's presence. "Jara." She hugged the old woman, who kissed her on the cheek and then held her at arm's length and examined her.

"You're looking well enough, I suppose," Jara said critically. "A little thin. Aren't you eating?"

Liothel laughed. No one had ever accused Jara of looking too thin, and she seemed to think everyone else should match her perpetual plumpness. "I'm fine. How was Innovar?"

Jara made a face. "Cold. Dull, too. And I don't mean just that old run-down wreck of a building they call a Wardfast. The students' heads were harder than the rocks in the walls. I don't think they learned a thing from me."

"That," Liothel said, "would be very hard for me to believe."

Jara chuckled, then noticed Kalia, standing in the doorway. "What's this? A new student?"

"Just for a day or two," said Liothel. "You won't get your hands on her full-time for a year or two. This is Kalia, our newest Acolyte. From Yvol's Hold."

Jara's face fell a little. "A bad business." But her expression quickly brightened again. "Well, lass," she told Kalia, "come in, come in. You may not know what we're talking about half the time, but that's all right—neither do your classmates!"

It took five minutes to settle the class enough for the lesson to begin after that remark.

The lesson was not one of those Liothel had trouble understanding—believing it was the problem. "But how can that be?" she demanded. "How can you have another world 'right next door'?"

"It can be that way because the Creator made it that way," Jara said, then held up her hand with a laugh as Liothel began an indignant response. "I know, that's like saying something is the way it is simply because that's the way it is. It's not really an answer. But it's the best I can do. We don't know how this is possible, but we know it's true."

"How can you even know that much?" another Acolyte demanded.

"We know it's true because Warders have been to this other world."

Kalia, who had been yawning in the corner, stiffened suddenly, her mouth closing with a snap. Liothel barely glanced at her, then turned back to Jara. "You just said nothing material can bridge the gap between the worlds. How could a Warder have been there?"

"They didn't travel with their bodies. Only their souls made the journey—their spirits."

"They went as ghosts?" protested another student.

"Oh, no. They had bodies."

"But—"

"They entered the minds of people in this other world."

"Like soulworms?" Liothel said in horror.

Jara nodded. "In a manner of speaking. But the Warders could not control the actions of their hosts like soulworms do—except in one strange case, where the Warder entered the body of a man similar to that poor mindless soul who came begging to our gate last Candleday. She was able to control his body as if it were her own, and she wandered that other world for several days and brought back reports of great wonders—cities as tall as the sky, lamps that burned without oil but were brighter than our finest lanterns, huge carriages that ran on endless roads of bright metal and belched black smoke. She was even able to speak to the people there, for the man could talk a little, and she found she could use his skills and memories as readily as her own."

"And this tale of hers was believed?" Liothel shook her head. "It must have been a dream."

"Her body remained here. The Sentinel confirmed her spirit was not in it, though it remained connected by a tenuous thread that led—elsewhere."

"But how was it done?" someone demanded. "And why have we never heard of it before?"

"The existence of this other world was discovered when a Sentinel, practicing her skill, reached out and touched a mind that seemed as close as the other side of the room—but she was alone. She had reached through to this other world through a weak place in the weft of the universe.

"It took her ten years to open that 'tear' so that a whole mind could go through it and explore what lay beyond. Once that was done, several Warders made the journey—though always one at a time, for the 'opening' between the worlds would only allow one link between a body in this universe and a soul in that one. In any event, that was a hundred years ago, and it has not been done since. Nor will it be done again."

"But why not?" Liothel asked. "I find it hard to believe any of this, Mistress, but I know you wouldn't lie to us, so it must be true. Why not go back? Who knows what could be learned from such a world?"

"No one has gone back because the hole between the worlds could not be closed," Jara said. "And in that other world—there are no soulworms."

Her class stared at her, including Kalia, who no longer looked the least bit tired or bored.

"Don't you see?" Jara went on. "That world was a violent place—all the Warders reported that. And it has more people than have lived in the whole history of this world. Were one soulworm to escape through the hole we have made, it would find the richest source of nourishment it could possibly imagine. It would breed, and its children would breed, and the violence in that other world would grow until millions had died. And all because we opened a gate that should not have been opened. We, the Warders, whose sole purpose is to protect the world from soulworms, would be responsible for introducing them to a world that does not know their horror."

"But the hole is there," Liothel whispered. "What is to prevent—"

"The hole is there. But the soulworms, even if they know it exists, cannot get to it. It is hidden, and guarded, and watched."

"I wish you hadn't told us this, Mistress," said one of the younger Acolytes solemnly, and Liothel had to agree.

"It is not pleasant knowledge," Jara concurred, "but it is necessary to know that Warders are as capable of making mistakes as the people we ward—and that, because of our responsibility, these mistakes have the potential of being far more disastrous than anything some foolish Prince Captain might do. We teach you about this greatest mistake of the Warders so that you will strive doubly hard to avoid the lesser mistakes. Think on these things, and learn."

With that formal phrase, she ended the lesson. She made the Warders' Sign and her students repeated it, then Liothel, with much to think about, turned to lead Kalia to the next class—and found the new Acolyte dozing once more in the corner.

4

Festival Day

In the waiting room of Weyburn General Hospital, a man and woman paced, held hands and talked in low voices, then paced some more. Styrofoam coffee cups piled up around them as the hands of the clock on the wall moved slowly from one to two to three a.m. When at last a green-garbed woman, mask hanging from her neck, emerged through the swinging doors marked "Surgery," they clung to each other like frightened children.

"She's out of danger," the doctor said; but she did not smile as she said it.

"Thank God!" said the man, but the woman, searching the doctor's face, said, "There's something wrong, isn't there?"

"There may be. Perhaps you should sit down..."

"What is this?" the man exploded. "You just said she's out of danger—"

"She's not going to die," the doctor said quietly. "But she should be awake by now—and she's not."

"I don't understand—"

The man's wife cut him off. "You're saying she's in a coma," she said, her voice little more than a whisper. "But there must be some hope—"

"There's always hope, Mrs. Gayle," said the doctor. "But right now that's all there is."

♌ ♌ ♌ ♌ ♌

Three days after Kalia came to Mykia, the expected batch of new Acolytes arrived, and she joined them for beginning instruction. For the next two weeks Liothel saw her only occasionally at meals and for a few minutes each night before the strictly enforced bedtime. She seemed happy, and was always friendly and cheerful around Liothel, but Liothel began to hear disturbing reports of her behavior elsewhere.

"...and then Kalia hit her, for no reason at all!" she overheard one of the new Acolytes tell another in the hall.

"I don't understand Kalia at all," the other said. "Most of the time she's really nice, but if someone crosses her...Shhh! It's the Old Lady!" Liothel's ears burned; she knew the younger Acolytes' nickname for her only too well, having heard it behind her back ever since Avondia Manifested, and she did not. She did her best to match the sweet smiles the two little girls gave her as she passed, but inside she fumed.

The remark about Kalia might have worried her more had it not been for the added insult to herself. But far more disturbing than either was to be called before the Acolyte Mother and Jara later that day.

"Come in, Liothel, come in," said the Mother absently. "And close the door behind you, there's a good girl." She looked down at her hands, folded on her lap.

Liothel complied and stood uncomfortably before the Mother's cluttered desk. Jara, seated by the fireplace to her left, smiled at her reassuringly. "Have I done something wrong, Mother?" Liothel blurted finally, when no one said anything.

The Acolyte Mother looked up and blinked. "Wrong? Oh, no, no, nothing like that. This meeting isn't really about you at all."

"It's about Kalia," said Jara. "She has been acting—strangely."

"You might say so," the Acolyte Mother said drily. "She struck another Acolyte in my class yesterday, Liothel, a little girl at least four years younger than she, and several times I have had to reprimand her for her unkind remarks, sometimes about the other Acolytes, sometimes even about Warders. You share a room with her; is there something troubling her?"

Liothel wondered for a moment where the Acolyte Mother had been when the young Acolytes were making unkind remarks about her. "I don't really see her much, but she's always been pleasant around me..." she said slowly. Then she frowned as memory niggled. "Except for the first day she was here—there was one outburst..."

"Outburst is a very good word for it," Jara said. "These incidents are always isolated, always short-lived...but taken together, they form a disturbing pattern."

"Disturbing, and disruptive," said the Acolyte Mother. "She must learn to control herself, or we shall have to expel her from the Keep."

"Oh, no!" Liothel protested, her words given more force by the guilty thought that if such a thing happened to herself, she wouldn't mind as much as she should. At least out there no one would despise her for being slow to reach her potential...but for Kalia, it was different. "This is all she has—"

"She could still remain in Mykia, as a worker below the Keep," the Mother said, but Liothel pictured herself shovelling out a stable and knew she would prefer exile to that. Kalia would surely feel the same way.... "We do not intend to put her out of the Wardfast. But here in the Keep we must have peace. Strife among the Acolytes cannot be tolerated. It could provide an opening in our defenses for the Enemy to exploit."

Liothel said nothing. There was no argument against that cold truth.

"We haven't done it yet," Jara pointed out with a small smile. "And we pray the Creator it won't be necessary. That's why we've called you here."

"I don't—"

"We want you to talk to her, explain what will happen if she cannot control herself. You know her better than anyone else; maybe she'll listen to you."

"It sounds like I don't really know her at all."

"But you'll try?"

Liothel nodded. "I'll try."

"Good girl!" Jara stood and hugged her. "It will all work out fine, you'll see."

Liothel returned her hug, but the absolute assurance she had felt as a little girl in Jara's arms was no longer there, and faded a little more each day as she failed to Manifest. Jara had told her often enough that that, too, would work out all right.

Sometimes, everything doesn't work out all right, she thought, leaving the office. *Jara would probably say realizing that is a sign I'm growing up...*she made a face. She knew she was growing up. That was her problem. She was growing up—but growing up without a Talent.

Kalia didn't have one either, not yet, but she was at the age where it could Manifest at any time. She had a future as a Warder, and Liothel wouldn't let her throw it away because she couldn't control her temper. That night, in the few minutes before bedtime, she sat on her bed and watched Kalia brushing her hair, which, though still short, had been neatly trimmed in the time since her arrival. "Kalia, is something wrong?" Liothel said at last.

Kalia didn't even glance at her. "Wrong?"

"I've heard—you've had some trouble in your classes."

Kalia stopped brushing. "Oh?"

"I'm worried about you."

"Really." Still holding the brush, she turned to face Liothel, her eyes hard and glittering in the candlelight.

"This kind of thing is very serious," Liothel hurried on. "You know enough about soulworms to know that any kind of violence or anger strengthens them and weakens us. The Warders can't allow it to go on."

"So they asked you to talk to me about it."

"Well...yes."

"Even though it's none of your business?" Kalia's voice had the harsh tone Liothel had heard once before, when, from atop the tower, they had seen the Verification party riding out. Her own temper rose in response.

"It is my business!" she snapped. "It's every Warder's business, because it threatens the Wardfast. If you can't learn to control your temper, Kalia, they'll throw you out of the Keep. You'll end up as a groom or gardener."

"Throw me out? Throw me out?" Kalia slammed the brush down on the table between the beds. "I almost died to get here! I walked for a month—starved—froze—hid from robbers—and now they want to throw me out?"

"They don't want to—but they will unless you learn—" Liothel realized she was shouting, stopped, and took a deep breath. "—to control yourself," she finished tightly.

"I'll—" Kalia began, then stopped. She closed her eyes for a long moment; when she opened them again, and spoke, her tone was gentler. "I'm sorry. It's just—the last few weeks haven't been easy for me. I'm still trying to adjust."

"Kalia, believe me, I understand. Things aren't always—easy—for me, either. Just—hold on to your temper, all right? For your sake. In a few days it will be Festival. No classes, lots of food, music—you'll feel like a new girl."

Kalia smiled a little. "I'm sure you're right." She twisted left, leaned forward and blew out the candle on the headboard of her bed. "Good night, Liothel." She lay down, pulled her blanket over her, and turned her back on her roommate.

Liothel stared at her. Just like that? She remembered what Jara had said about Kalia's outbursts—always sudden, always short-lived. Liothel's own not-inconsiderable temper was like that, too, but even she wouldn't have cooled down as quickly as Kalia just had. And certainly she wouldn't have been ready to go to sleep immediately afterward. She snuffed out her own candle and lay down, remembering that first day when Kalia had appeared, how Avondia and Maris had quarrelled about something, how she herself had felt about the girl, the sudden surge of anger on the tower. It all left her with a faint sense of unease that followed her down into restless sleep.

In the morning she dismissed the feeling as the product of a bad day and reported her conversation with Kalia to the Acolyte Mother. A few days later Jara told her Kalia had settled down admirably. There were no more incidents.

Even if there had been, Liothel thought shortly afterward as she hung evergreen boughs above the doorways of the Great Hall, probably no one would have noticed in the usual pre-Festival madness. Warders of course could not permit themselves to lose their tempers (though Liothel sometimes wondered how many tantrums were later thrown behind closed doors), but the level of politeness rose dramatically, a sure sign of fraying patience.

Festival Day dawned gray and cold, with a thin, sleet-like snow sifting from the leaden sky. But the Acolytes rose long before the sun made any impression on the overcast—it was their task to prepare the Hall for the Great Ceremony and the feast that would follow it. In response to the clanging of the morning bell in the Acolyte Hall, Liothel swung her feet out of bed, immediately broke out in goosebumps, and dressed as quickly as she could. Even so, Kalia was waiting impatiently by the door before Liothel finished lacing her right shoe.

"First time I ever saw you get out of bed in a hurry on a cold morning," Liothel grumbled as she joined her roommate.

"But today's the big day, isn't it?" Kalia said with an enigmatic smile. "Festival."

"As far as I'm concerned, Festival Day's just a lot of work. It's the next four days I'm looking forward to—no duties!"

Kalia laughed. The sound grated oddly on Liothel's nerves. She berated herself for her reaction. *That's no way to start the Festival*, she thought.

They gathered with the other Acolytes in the Great Hall, and after a hurried breakfast of porridge, began the preparations. Each of them first donned a sea-green tabard edged with silver, then moved on to a pre-assigned task, Liothel's being to light the big lamps inside globes of colored glass that had been hung from every beam during the past week, while Kalia helped bring in the Festival chairs for the Inner Circle, massive thrones of gilded wood and red velvet that replaced the usual plain white ones at the table on the dais. Then together they reported to the kitchen to peel potatoes.

Other Acolytes scurried around on their own duties, and though with only an hour to go until the start of the Great Ceremony it appeared impossible that everything would be ready on time, when the chimes rang through the Keep summoning everyone to the Great Hall, the silver and crystal settings glittered on the tables, roast pork wafted its savory scent throughout the room, mingling with the fresh smell of evergreen, and everything glowed in the light of the colored lamps and the thousands of candles around the chamber.

The Warders filed solemnly in and took their places at the long tables, then the Inner Circle entered, led by Guardian Mother Amaryl, bearing the Light of Prisca, a silver-and-crystal lantern that legend said had been lit by the First Warder herself and never allowed to go out. Amaryl set the Light on a stand behind her throne, where its pure white illumination, so different from the soft light of the candles and colored lamps, brought brilliant life to the silver-and-green tapestry of Prisca, looking down on her followers with eyes that seemed almost alive.

Then the Guardian Mother turned to face the gathered Warders and Acolytes and began the Great Ceremony. Through the songs and prayers and recitations that followed, Liothel kept her eyes on the tapestry, hearing the old story of the First Warder and her battle with the Great Worm as if for the first time, and for the moment, at least, there was nowhere she would rather have been, Talent or no Talent.

Once she made the Warders' Sign following the final phrase of the final prayer, however, she had to plunge back into the everyday concern of getting the enormous quantity of food in the kitchen distributed to the hungry Warders in the Hall. They had gone without breakfast in preparation for the ceremony.

She was refilling a water cup near the front of the Hall when, out of the corner of her eye, she saw Kalia slip out into the hallway. On her way back to the kitchen she glanced through the door in time to see Kalia jerk the green tabard over her head and throw it almost angrily behind a cabinet, then dash down the corridor.

Every vague foreboding Kalia had ever engendered in Liothel returned ten times stronger. She put down the water pitcher and ran after the other girl.

But as Kalia had shown at the baths her first day in Mykia, she was faster than Liothel, who fell farther and farther behind. Still, she couldn't lose her; the hallway they followed led to only one place: the Tower.

Liothel's foreboding waxed into fear as a terrible awareness grew in her, a knowledge almost too horrible to bear. Bits of remembered conversation flashed through her mind: "...only a tinge of darkness on the fifth level..." "...they thrive on the negative emotions, anger, lust, and hate...they infiltrate their victims, influence their actions..." "...it is our greatest dread that one day a soulworm will infiltrate a Wardfast..."

And then Liothel's fear turned to pure, almost blinding, terror, as an image appeared in her mind, the image of Kalia's sudden intense interest as Jara told them of the gate to another world, the gate that opened from within Mykia—within the Tower—

Kalia looked back for the first time, from the far end of the long, tapestry-hung hall she and Liothel had gone down that first day, and laughed, her girl's voice overlaid with some harsher tone that screeched in Liothel's ears and mind. Then she ducked through the arch into the Tower, and a child screamed, the shrill sound ending abruptly, and Liothel remembered it was traditional to place one of the newest Acolytes at the Tower's entrance as a "guard" during the Great Ceremony. "Oh, no!" she gasped with what little breath she still had. "No!"

But when she reached the arch she stopped as though she had hit a wall, staggered back, turned and retched up what was left of her long-ago breakfast, though even with her eyes closed she could still see in sickening detail the body of the child in Acolyte's gray at the foot of the stairs, her head twisted unnaturally, her face frozen in mute astonishment, and blood staining her lips...

Furiously Liothel drove herself to her feet, ignoring the weakness. She had to stop Kalia, had to—

But of course it was too late, had been too late from the beginning. As always she cracked her head as she entered the Tower, but she ignored the pain and mounted the stairs, forcing herself to step over the dead Acolyte. She climbed past landing after landing, closed door after closed door, until at last she came to one that wasn't closed, and through which flooded flickering blue light that hurt her eyes.

Kalia stood on the other side of an intricate design incised in the stone floor of the empty room. From the centre of that design crackled the otherwordly illumination, turning Kalia's face the color of late-winter ice—but her eyes burned, and her voice dripped scorching hatred. "You can have this world, Warder. But this one—" she pointed at the eye-paining hole— "this one is mine!"

Liothel knew she should rush into the room, drive Kalia away, knock her down—but her feet felt rooted to the floor. With a last, screeching laugh, Kalia squatted and slapped her hand against the pattern.

And then she screamed, like the Acolyte she had killed, the sound of a child in mortal terror, no trace in it of the harsh shriek of the soulworm; and that sound, at last, drove Liothel forward—or would have, if strong hands had not seized her from behind, held her back as Kalia screamed and kept on screaming, then suddenly collapsed like a puppet whose strings had been cut, her hand still thrust into the pattern, whose light faded to a dim blue glow.

Liothel heard someone's breath catch in their throat, and it might have been hers, but wasn't. She looked around wildly, to see Jara, Guardian Mother Amaryl, Apprentice

40

Sentinel Avondia, Warrior Mother Isildor and Exorcist Mother Yvandel all standing behind her, all staring with blank, shocked faces at the room before them. The hands that held her slackened their grip and fell away, and she turned to see Sharkon, the Warrior who had accompanied the Verification Party to Yvol's Hold.

It was from the Warrior's throat, Liothel realized, that half-sob had come, and somehow that, more than anything else, made her realize the unthinkable really had happened:

The Enemy had entered a new world...and the Warders had opened the door.

5

A Warder's Duty

The doctor, making her rounds, stopped to look in on Maribeth Gayle in the room that had been dubbed by the nurses and interns, not unkindly, "Sleeping Beauty's Castle." She took the clipboard from the end of the bed, then glanced at the steadily beeping heart monitor. "No change in the past twenty-four hours?" she asked the nurse accompanying her.

"No, doctor." The nurse looked down at the girl's peaceful face. "It's spooky. You'd swear she was just sleeping."

The doctor made a notation on the chart. "As far as I can tell, she is. I can't find a thing wrong with her. Even those brain scans we had done in Saskatoon turned up nothing." She put the clipboard back on its hook and watched the steady rise and fall of the girl's chest. "You want to know what's really spooky?" she said after a moment. "The other girl from the accident."

"Oh, yes, I remember her. Christine—what was her last name—Redpath? Was that it?" She gave the doctor a curious glance. "But she was hardly hurt at all."

"Not physically. But something happened—up here." The doctor tapped her temple. "She's functioning, but more like a robot than a human being. It's like there's nobody home inside her head—as if Christine has packed up and left her body behind." She nodded at Maribeth. "Which appears to be exactly what she's done, only more thoroughly." She sighed and turned away to continue her rounds. "Sometimes I wonder if either one of them will ever find her way back."

𝔏 𝔏 𝔏 𝔏 𝔏

Two hours after the soulworm's escape, those who had witnessed it gathered in the Guardian Mother's chambers, very near the Tower, to discuss what was to be done. Kalia lay unconscious in the infirmary, and the healers feared she would never wake. Though she had been possessed for only a few weeks, the wrench of the soulworm fleeing through her into another world had been a terrible shock, and rather than recover, her mind might simply quit—and shortly thereafter, her body.

The Acolyte the soulworm had killed was hidden away until the morrow, Amaryl having decreed that news of the disaster was not to be spread among the other Warders until the day after Festival. "Let them have their revelry," she said. "What damage the soulworm could do in this world has been done. What must now concern us is the damage it could do in that other world."

Avondia was the last of the witnesses to arrive at the Guardian Mother's chambers; she was accompanied by Blind Maris. Liothel, already miserable, almost gasped with shock when she saw the Sentinel. For the first time, Maris looked truly old—old and worn out, as though something vital had been drained from her body.

Amaryl greeted her gravely, then bolted the door and motioned the members of the Inner Circle to take seats around the large oval table in the innermost room. Avondia took a chair beside but slightly behind Maris; Liothel sat on a low bench along one wall and wished she was somewhere else.

"When I summoned you so abruptly from the feast—all of you except Liothel, who had already realized something of the truth—you had to be content with my bald statement

43

that a soulworm was loose in the Wardfast," Amaryl said. "Before we discuss what happens next, I think Sharkon should tell you what she told me." She nodded to the Warrior.

"I shall be brief, Guardian Mother," Sharkon said. "The Verification Party found Yvol's Hold destroyed, just as Kalia told us. But there was more than human cruelty at work, for Tiella felt at once the spoor of the soulworm-possessed, as strongly as she has ever felt it anywhere: soulworms had spawned there.

"We tracked the new worms to a group of five survivors in the ruins of a nearby farm. They were weak with hunger, and therefore offered little physical resistance and were easily exorcised by Esbania. The worms I destroyed with fire, and Tiella said the five survivors should recover completely.

"But they were not all the survivors, nor all the possessed. After the exorcism, we learned that there had been another—a young girl, Kalia. I rode back here at once—almost killed my horse—and yet arrived too late." Her tone as she finished was bitter.

"You are not to blame for the limitations the Creator has placed upon horse and woman," Guardian Mother Amaryl said gently.

"No," Blind Maris said. The word seemed to thud on the table like a stone. No one wanted to look at her; yet each could not help it. She sat upright, stern-faced, blank eyes staring straight ahead—but Liothel could see her trembling. "You are not to blame for anything, Sharkon. The blame is mine."

"Mistress..." Avondia touched Maris's hand, but the Sentinel pulled it free and held it up. It shook.

"The fault for this intrusion into the Wardfast is entirely my own," she said, her voice like gravel grinding between millstones. "When I Tested Kalia, Avondia said she thought

44

she felt a hint of darkness on the fifth level. I discounted it, because I hadn't felt it." Her voice grew even grimmer. "But it's worse than that. Creator help me, I knew—I knew—I hadn't reached the fifth level. I was barely able to penetrate to the fourth."

"The fourth is not deep enough for a true Testing," Amaryl said slowly, as though trying to understand.

"I know!" Maris cried. Her hand clenched and she slammed it against the table. "I know!" Her voice dropped to a harsh whisper. "My Gift is deserting me, Guardian Mother! I didn't want to admit it, so I pretended—even to myself—my Apprentice was wrong. I have let a soulworm into Mykia!" Tears ran from her blind eyes down her withered cheeks, but when Avondia tried again to take her hand, she pulled it free almost violently.

"What's done is done," said Amaryl. "Maris, I share your pain—more than you know. The security of the Wardfast is mine to maintain. The soulworm should not have been able to get inside—granted. But once inside, it should not have been able to get a key to the Tower room of the Gate—and it should not have been faced with only a—" Her voice caught; she swallowed and pressed on, "—a twelve-year-old girl as a guard. We have grown complacent, Warders. It has cost us." She reached across the table and laid her hand on Maris's, and from her touch, Maris did not draw away. "It has cost all of us."

"I hereby resign as Sentinel," whispered Maris. "As I should have done months ago. Avondia—"

"Mistress?"

"Mistress no longer. From this moment, you are the Sentinel." She stood, no longer trembling, but looking as old as Mykia's weathered stones. "If someone will guide me to the door, I will leave the Inner Circle to continue its deliberations."

45

Liothel blinked back tears, and looked at Amaryl. Surely the Guardian Mother wouldn't let Maris...

But Amaryl only nodded, though her own eyes were bright. "Sentinel Avondia," she said. "Please aid Warder Maris."

Liothel watched the new Sentinel (*Sentinel! And she's no older than I am!*) guide the blind woman to the door, and wondered if she shouldn't resign as well—resign as Acolyte, leave the Wardfast, give up on her supposed Talent. For two weeks—two weeks—she had lived in a room with a soulworm-possessed girl, and never suspected. And when at last she had suspected, when only a—a fool (she had started to think, "only a blind woman," but that thought hurt too much) could still have been misled, she had been too slow, too slow to stop Kalia from killing a little girl, too slow—or too scared (she remembered with shame how her feet had refused to move) to stop the soulworm from invading another world. Too slow. Too slow to Manifest, too slow to learn, too slow to understand, too slow to act. Too slow to be a Warder.

Avondia returned to the table and sat in Maris's old seat, face white, spine stiff. Liothel saw her swallow, hard.

"Now," Amaryl said. "We have let a soulworm into the Wardfast, and that soulworm has let itself out into another world through that door created by our predecessors. What we of the Inner Circle must decide is—what do we do to correct this great evil?"

"We know what the records show," said Jara. "That world is a violent place. The soulworm will spawn, and the people of that world will be unable to either detect or defeat its kind. Their society will dissolve into chaos and war, as did our own before the advent of Prisca."

"But the records are a hundred years old," argued Exorcist Mother Yvandal. "Perhaps they have learned peace."

"Then the soulworm will create the violence it requires, using whatever person it has possessed. It will take longer, but the end will be the same."

"There is nothing to debate," Warrior Mother Isildor said sternly. "Our duty is unmistakeable. We must go after it, exorcise it and destroy it before it reproduces."

Silence fell. Isildor had given voice to what they all knew to be true—a Warder would have to do what had not been done for a century, travel into that other world, and somehow find and face the soulworm. Though the world that was threatened wasn't their own, duty compelled them, for they had opened the Gate.

Finally Amaryl sighed. "Isildor is right, of course. But whom do we send?"

Jara, who had been sitting with head bowed, looked up slowly. "The answer to that question is as clear as was the other." Her gaze travelled around the table. "It must be me."

Liothel jerked upright. "No!"

A single glance from Amaryl choked off her protest. Jara didn't even look at her. "We can only send one person; the ancient records make that clear. Only one link between the body on this side of the Gate and the other world can be maintained. The soulworm has not blocked the Gate for us because it transferred its entire physical existence; it has no link back through the Gate to this world. We cannot do that. We can only send a mind—one mind. But it takes three skills to destroy a soulworm: Detection, Exorcism and Warring. I am the only double-talented Warder in Mykia, and like all of us, I have some training in the skills of a Warrior. No one else can do what must be done."

"Your skills may not even transfer to your host, whoever that may be," Amaryl warned. "You may be only a helpless spectator."

"Then our neighboring world is lost," said Jara flatly.

Silence, again. The Warders exchanged looks. Liothel held her breath. Finally Amaryl spoke. "Agreed."

Liothel stared at Jara, the woman closest to being the mother she had never known, and felt a pang in her heart as though she had already lost her.

6

Into The Flames

In the late-night semi-darkness of her hospital room, Maribeth lay as she always lay, her breathing slow and deep, the phosphorescent trace of her heartbeat on the monitor strong and steady.

At her station down the hall, the nurse watching the half-dozen monitors looked away from them to finish filling out her log before the change of shift. She didn't see the sudden speeding of Maribeth's pulse; nor was there anyone in Maribeth's room to see her eyes flicker and her fingers twitch spasmodically.

A moment later, everything was as it had been; and when the nurse looked up after only two or three minutes of inattention, Maribeth's heart had resumed the measured pace of someone whose deep sleep is untroubled by dreams.

ᘒ   ᘒ   ᘒ   ᘒ   ᘒ

Despite the urgency, the Warders could do nothing at once to pursue their enemy. They weren't soulworms; Jara could not crash through the Gate and take control of the first person she contacted. Like the long-ago Warder Jara had spoken of in class, they had to find someone whose mind was feeble, someone whose body Jara could manipulate freely—though the questionable morality of that in itself sparked long debates all over Mykia.

For three days various Detectors sent thought-tendrils through the Gate, delicately reaching into the minds of people on the far side, always in fear of touching the one the soulworm had possessed and thus betraying their presence. That didn't happen; and remarkably, repeatedly, they touched a mind that seemed to be just what they needed.

"We all agree," Jara told Liothel late one evening. Liothel had taken to spending as much time as possible with the tutor, for her heart was filled with fear she would never see her whole again. They sat in Jara's chambers, on cushions beside the fire, while the worst snowstorm of the winter, driven by a bitter northwest wind, lashed the shuttered window. "The mind is whole, and the body is whole, but the personality is elsewhere, driven deep by some trauma, perhaps. Whatever, it is perfect for our purposes."

"It? Is it a man or woman?"

"It—I mean, she—" Jara smiled slightly, "is a girl." She laughed softly. "I've never been one of those old people who spend all their time wishing they were young again, but it looks like I'm going to get that wish."

Liothel slowly turned her warm mug of blueberry tea this way and that, watching the firelight play off the pale blue liquid. "But what—what if you lose yourself?"

"Hmm?"

"What if you can't find your way back? What then?" Liothel looked up, a lump in her throat. "Jara, you're the closest thing to a mother I have. If I lost you—"

Jara reached out and touched her cheek. "But you will lose me, sooner or later," she said gently. "I am not terribly old, but neither am I young, and though I expect to have many more years with you, the Creator gives us no assurance of that. Do I stop doing what must be done just to prolong my own life? That would be selfish, indeed. If I die in this task, then at least I will die doing what I have dedicated my life to doing—serving the Creator by fighting the Enemy."

"If you can. It may not even be possible, in that other world!"

"The soulworm is a physical being, though on a different plane than ours, one we don't fully understand. Obviously it is not material as we are material, for we cannot travel bodily through the Gate, as it has. Nevertheless, we know that fire disrupts its existence. Whatever happens to my Gifts, that knowledge will remain."

"But if you can't Exorcise it, you'd have to..." Liothel's voice trailed off.

Jara looked away. "I see you understand."

"Could you do that?" Liothel whispered. "Could you really burn its host to destroy it?"

Jara still didn't look at her. "Now you ask the question I have asked myself every minute of every day since this task was set me. Liothel...I don't know. I hope I could, to save a world. I hope I would have the strength—and that the Creator would forgive me."

Liothel, staring into the fire, seemed to see a woman writhing in pain. She closed her eyes. "But if you could not Detect, either..."

"Then I would have to look for other signs of the soulworm's presence. It will not be as subtle there as it was here, for it will think it has no Warders to fear. Its host will almost certainly exhibit a radical change of personality—and will be striving to create the violent, negative emotions it feeds on, leading eventually to an explosion of physical violence when it spawns. I would watch as long as I dared, and then—do what has to be done."

Liothel opened her eyes again and met Jara's calm blue ones. "But what if you were wrong?"

Jara's voice was steady. "Then I would indeed hope that I never came back."

They were both quiet for a long time. Liothel looked into the fire again. *Jara would not have hesitated,* she thought bitterly. *Jara would not have stood and watched as the soulworm entered the Gate. She would have stopped it, somehow, some way...*

She's a Warder. I'm just an Acolyte—the Old Lady Acolyte. The one who may never be a Warder. "What am I doing here?"

She didn't realize she had spoken aloud until Jara said, "Letting your tea go cold?"

"No." Liothel suddenly turned toward Jara. "I mean, what am I doing here, in Mykia?"

The smile Jara had been trying on faded. "Becoming a Warder."

"A Warder? Me?" Liothel gestured at her gray robe. "I'm an Acolyte. I'm an Acolyte two years older than any Acolyte Mykia has ever seen. I'm an Acolyte, and the only other girl my age was just named Sentinel! I'm an Acolyte so old that the other Acolytes call me names behind my back. What am I doing here?"

"You have a Talent. It will manifest. Just give it time."

"A Talent?" Liothel laughed bitterly. "A Talent? Maris told me I have a Talent. Maybe she was wrong about that, too!"

Jara's expression tightened. "Liothel, that's unkind."

"I think I have manifested my Talent! I have a Talent for stupidity, for missing the obvious, for failing. That is my Talent!"

Jara, eyes wide, put down her mug and leaned forward to say something, but Liothel didn't give her the chance. All her frustration and anger at herself was pouring out and she could no longer stem the flood. "I've lived in Mykia all my life—all my life—and for what? So I could stand and watch a soulworm mock us all, and never lift a finger to stop it? All my life I've waited to become a Warder, to prove I'm worth something, to prove you were right to take me in—to prove it's all been worthwhile living here, with no family, no real friends, no—no—" To her horror, she realized she was crying. She slammed the mug down on the floor so hard it shattered. Hot tea splashed across the cushions and hissed in the fire. Liothel lunged to her feet and would have fled the room if Jara hadn't grabbed her arm.

"Liothel, stop it! Shh! Shh!" Jara hugged her tight, and Liothel, almost unwillingly, felt her tense muscles relax, until finally she was sobbing on Jara's shoulder. The older woman led her to the couch. "I had no idea—what do you think you could have done to stop Kalia?"

"I could have pushed her away from the Gate. I could have...I don't know. But I never even tried!"

"You would have had to cross the Gate yourself, and if you had, your spirit would be in that other world, defenseless against the soulworm, and we would be unable to fight it. You did all you could."

"But it wasn't enough! And before that, I lived with Kalia all those weeks, I should have realized—"

"Child, the soulworm was very, very cautious. Most of the time Kalia was Kalia, or very much like her—just a girl. Only rarely did the soulworm take complete control of her. It was frightened, wary. It fooled all of us. It fooled the Sentinel, Liothel. How were you to know?"

"But—"

"Listen to me. You're not to blame—not any more than the rest of us. All of us share some of the responsibility. But very little of it is yours. Do you hear me?"

Liothel swallowed. "I—guess so."

"As for the other..." Jara sighed. "I know it's been hard on you, Liothel. You see these Acolytes come here with tales of their homes and families, their normal, everyday lives, and you envy them. The only thing that you have is your hope of becoming a Warder—and that seems to be taking forever. I understand your frustration. But you mustn't give up. Your Talent is there, inside you. It will come out. It must."

Liothel wished she could believe Jara fully—but in her heart, she still doubted. "Jara, you have to come back to me," she pleaded. "You're the only real friend I've got. If something happens—if you don't—I won't be able to stay. I won't!"

Jara hugged her again. "Don't make any rash promises, child," she whispered. "Don't."

A log cracked loudly in the fire.

There was fire, too, in the chamber of the Gate two days later, when the somber Inner Circle, and Liothel, gathered for the ceremony that would send Jara on her way. The Guardian Mother had wanted to bar Liothel from the ritual, but Jara had intervened. "She is my friend," she told Amaryl. "And she has been a part of this tale since the beginning. She deserves to see how it ends."

Amaryl had relented reluctantly, and Liothel almost wished she hadn't, for before going to the chamber she had visited Kalia, lying motionless between linen sheets. Outside the sun shone on wind-carved drifts of snow, reflecting so much light through the infirmary window the room was painfully bright, and Kalia, pale and thinner than ever, looked almost transparent. Liothel sat with her for a time, thinking of the girl she had thought she was beginning to know, and wondering what, if anything, was left of her—and wondering, too, how much of what she had seen in Kalia had been Kalia and how much of it had been the creature that had been using her.

And then she thought of Jara lying there just as thin and white, and she wished again she knew nothing of what was about to take place.

But nevertheless she was there when Jara entered the chamber and lay down on the bed that had been placed beside the Gate. Its blue glare had faded to a faint glow barely perceptible in the light of the candles ringing the room. Since the decision had been made to pursue the soulworm, a trench had been cut in the stone of the floor at the base of the wall. Warrior Mother Isildor poured the last of a jar of clear green oil into it, then stepped outside, turned and spoke to Jara. "When you begin, I will light the Circle of Fire, to burn until you return. Should the soulworm flee back through the Gate during the transfer, the Circle will contain it, and I will destroy it."

Jara nodded and lay back on the bed. "The Creator be with us all, friends," she murmured, closed her eyes, and reached out to touch the pattern.

Its glow strengthened at once, and at the same instant Isildor stepped forward and touched a torch to the oil. Fire leaped high and higher, ringing the room. Liothel moved as close to the flames in the doorway as she could. Through their flickering screen of light she could see the blue glow waxing, pouring out of the incised pattern. *The Creator protect you, Jara,* Liothel thought. *May He bring you back to—*

Her prayer broke off in sudden terror as she saw flames rushing across the floor. Some hidden crack in the stone, unseen by those who had so hurriedly dug the trench, had filled with oil, making a fuse leading straight to the bed. Even as Liothel realized what that meant, a corner of Jara's robe, touching the floor, burst into flame.

"No!" Liothel screamed, and without even thinking, leaped forward. A moment of searing heat and she was through the wall of flame, shouts ringing out behind her. She dashed across the floor and seized Jara's robe in both hands, ripping it from her with such force Jara's hand was pulled from the emblem and Liothel tripped and fell, flinging the burning garment away from her.

She twisted, trying to catch herself, and had a momentary, horrifying glimpse of the blue emblem, now flaring as brightly as it had the day the soulworm went through, before her head struck the floor at its centre. The blue seemed to stab deep into her eyes and she screamed.

But an instant later she couldn't hear her scream, or anything else. She seemed to sink below her body, seeing it above her on the floor of the tower, now as transparent as glass, glass that blurred and ran together into fog that blew away in a cold wind from nowhere—and then she fell.

Tumbling, screaming silently, she plunged toward a point of malevolent red light that suddenly flared and swelled into an enormous pool of fire, reaching hungrily for her with long red tongues. The flames filled her vision and her mind until nothing else was left—then vanished into darkness, and took her consciousness with them.

7

Sleeping Beauty

Light. It seeped through her eyelids against her will. *The fire!* she thought, but that had been green—no, red—and this was white. White, like daylight, only softer...

Fluorescent. Fluorescent light, her mind whispered, and suddenly her eyes opened and she stared up at it, a big rectangular panel glowing with honest, familiar, magical (magical?) fluorescent light.

She blinked again. *Of course, fluorescent. Nothing magical about it. But why was it there? This wasn't her room. And what was that beeping sound?*

Infirmary, she thought, then frowned slightly, still staring at the light. *No, that wasn't the right word. It was a—a hospital, that was it. She must be in a hospital. There had been an accident. She had fallen and hit her—no, something worse than that. But what?*

She tried to remember, but her thoughts swirled uselessly. *She'd been at a party—something to do with—with—a festival? No, of course not, where had that come from? A birthday, or—or something. A boy—Tom Eston—and a girl, Kal—Ka—Christine. Her best friend, Christine Redpath. They had gone for a ride out in the country, and...and then everything was blank until she woke here.*

We must have crashed, she thought. *Hit something, or rolled, or...but why can't I remember it? What happened to Tom and Christine? How bad am I hurt?*

She tried to sit up but couldn't, and felt a moment of blind panic. *I'm paralyzed!* Then she realized there were restraints holding her down, and finally she looked around her.

To her left a heart monitor, hung on a chrome stand, made the beeping noise that had puzzled her. A wire ran from it to her, and she was suddenly very aware of several sore spots on her chest where leads were attached. For a moment she watched the jagged blue line traced by her heartbeat; then she looked beyond it at the window, green curtains drawn wide but revealing nothing but a rectangular swath of blue sky.

Slowly, because the room twirled around her when she moved too quickly, she turned her head the other way and identified the vague discomfort in her right arm as a needle feeding a slow drip of liquid into her veins from a glass vial suspended on another silvery pole. Beyond that squatted an ugly green vinyl-covered chair, pushed up against the wall, and an open door through which gleamed a blue-and-white tiled floor. A nurse carrying a clipboard hurried past without looking in.

The girl looked at the foot of the bed, then, and saw, over the twin humps of her feet beneath the blankets (*At least they didn't cut anything off!* she thought, and wriggled her toes to prove it), a table covered with flowers and cards and a small television on a swinging arm of gray metal. Hanging above it, across the width of the room, a banner commanded her in green spray paint to "Get Well Soon!" Dozens of ballpoint and felt-pen signatures covered the unpainted cloth; the tape holding it in place had given way in one corner, resulting in a dog-ear that hid part of the exclamation point.

She stared at it for a long time, then surveyed the rest of the room again. Nothing changed. The blue line of the monitor continued to prove that her heart still pumped. Glowing red numbers counted her pulse: 64. 65. 63. 64.

They must have tied me down so I wouldn't roll over in my sleep and pull out the needle, she thought. *Now how am I supposed to call the nurse?*

But a few minutes later, just as though she had reached the call button, a nurse appeared in the door, her head turned away as she spoke to someone in the hallway. She held a tall, slender vase of white glass with a single long-stemmed rose in it. "...it's not as if the poor girl can appreciate all these flowers..."

"But it's lovely," the girl said, or tried to. It came out in a hoarse whisper, but the nurse undoubtedly heard it—the vase crashed to the floor as she whirled to face the bed. For a moment she stared, then made a choked cry, punched a button on the intercom by the door and shouted, "Dr. Ryback to Room 302, Dr. Ryback to Room 302!"

Another nurse appeared in the doorway, and then another, and then a couple of men in pajamas and robes who craned their necks to see what everyone was staring at. But they were chivvied away a moment later by a woman in a white coat, who turned to the nurse who had dropped the vase and asked, "What's going—"

The nurse pointed mutely; the doctor looked, blinked, looked again, and said, "Well, I'll be—" She grinned broadly and came over to the bed. "Welcome back, Maribeth."

*Maribeth? That didn't sound quite right...*but then suddenly, as though she had been watching a fuzzy television picture and someone had just fine-tuned it, the strange confusion and uncertainty that had gripped her since she woke vanished. *Of course her name was Maribeth—Maribeth Gayle, sixteen years old, a Grade 11 student at Weyburn Comprehensive School. Go, Eagles!*

She managed to smile at Dr. Ryback, remembering the only other time she had been in hospital, when her tonsils had been taken out. "Where's my ice cream, Doctor?" she whispered, and Dr. Ryback, after a moment of blankness, suddenly laughed with delight.

"Nothing wrong with your memory, anyway!"

Maribeth's smile faded. "Then why can't I remember why I'm here?"

Dr. Ryback's own smile disappeared. "What's the last thing you do remember?"

"Tom Eston and Christine Redpath and I were at a party. We left to take a drive in Tom's new car.... Was there an accident?"

"Yes. And we were worried about you for a while. But you're going to be fine now." Dr. Ryback turned away. "I'm going to call your parents. They'll be thrilled—"

Maribeth blinked. Her parents. *Why weren't they there? If she'd been in the hospital for a day or two, or even a week, she was sure at least one of them would have been there whenever it was allowed. Unless...*

"How long have I been here?"

Dr. Ryback paused in the doorway, and exchanged glances with the nurse, who had swept up the broken glass from the vase and now froze with the dustpan over the waste basket. "I think you should rest right now," the doctor said. "We can talk later..." The glass clattered into the basket.

"Dr. Ryback, please. How long?"

Dr. Ryback hesitated again, then finally sighed and turned to meet her patient's eyes. "You've been in a coma for almost two months."

Maribeth's head whirled. "That's not possible..."

"I'm afraid it's true." Dr. Ryback hesitated, then said, "I'll call your parents," and went out.

The nurse came over to the bed and began unbuckling the restraints. "Well, we won't need these any more, will we? Just try not to move around too much—not that I imagine you're really up to it, after all this time in bed..." She chattered on while she worked, but Maribeth hardly heard her. *The party had been...to celebrate the football team's victory over the Usher Unicorns. Tom was a football player. It had been October 15, she remembered the date clearly. So now it must be...*

"Well, this is certainly going to be a merry Christmas for your parents, I can tell you that!" said the nurse.

Dr. Ryback returned. "They're on their way. But I'm only going to let them in for a few minutes, then you'll have to rest. There's a big difference between natural sleep and what you've been doing for the past two months."

Something almost held Maribeth back from asking the next question. She was afraid she didn't want to know the answer. "What happened to Tom and Christine?"

Again the doctor and nurse looked at each other. "I really think we should talk about this later..."

The blue line on the monitor wobbled as Maribeth's heart skipped. "They're dead!" *Fire...*

"No!" Dr. Ryback came quickly to her side. "Not both of them."

"What do you mean, not both?" Maribeth cried.

The doctor took a deep breath. "The boy—Tom Eston. He died at the scene. Your friend, Christine, had some bruises and cuts, but she's fine now." She patted Maribeth's hand. "Just like you will be. You had a couple of broken bones, but they've had plenty of time to heal."

"Tom..."

"I don't want you brooding about it." Dr. Ryback smoothed Maribeth's hair back from her forehead with gentle fingers. "You should rest until your parents get here."

"But—"

"No buts!" The doctor ushered the nurse out the door, but paused for a moment before leaving. "I'm sorry about your friend," she said in a low voice. "I know what it's like to lose one." Her tone brightened. "But the important thing now is your health. We'll have to strengthen you up a bit, and run a few tests to make sure everything is functioning normally, then we'll send you home. We need these beds for sick people, you know!" She smiled again, then went out.

Maribeth stared up at the light panel that had been her first sight on awakening—after two months. Two months...and Tom, dead? She hadn't known him that well, but he'd been Christine's boyfriend...*how had she taken it? It must have torn her up inside,* she thought. *I hope she'll come see me...*

Somehow in the next few minutes she drifted to sleep, but woke to a gentle touch on her arm and opened her eyes to see a man and woman, both wearing winter clothing, looking down at her with eyes wide and bright with tears. She blinked at them. They looked almost familiar, but...

That strange click into focus repeated. "Mom! Dad!" Tears sprang to her own eyes. She was too weak to throw her arms around them the way she wanted to, and the I.V. would have prevented it in any case, but her parents hugged her the best they could. The warmth of their arms around her broke something open inside her, and she sobbed.

Yet even as they held her, a small voice of terror whispered deep inside her, *You didn't recognize your own parents. What's happened to you?*

She didn't have an answer, but as her mother wiped the tears from her face with trembling fingers and her father kissed her forehead, she didn't need one.

For the moment, love was enough.

CHAPTER 8

Home Again

When Maribeth woke the morning of the day after she had regained consciousness, disorientation gripped her again for a few seconds, so that she stared at the fluorescent light as though she had never seen it before, and shied away from the beeping monitor. Everything seemed too smooth, too bright, too strange. But by the time the nurse arrived to perform the morning ritual of blood pressure, temperature and pulse, she felt herself again—except for that little core of fear inside her, fear that she had been hurt worse than the doctors' tests had shown, that these periods of confusion were the symptom of some hidden brain damage.

But the episode did not repeat itself that day, and the next morning she felt no more mixed up than she normally did on awakening. As the rest of the week passed without the problem recurring, she decided it had been nothing more than a passing side-effect of being unconscious for two months. She didn't mention it to Dr. Ryback.

Her parents returned at frequent intervals, in between the dozens of tests Dr. Ryback insisted on performing. Maribeth's mother in particular looked at her almost hungrily, as though she could hardly believe she was there and awake, and chattered on and on about everything that had happened while Maribeth had been unconscious.

But while Maribeth soon knew every detail of what the dog had been up to, and how her little brother Sean (who was away at a week-long hockey tournament) was doing in math, she noticed that her mother never said a word about

Christine Redpath. Finally she interrupted a monologue about Sean's Christmas play to ask, "Mom, have you seen Christine recently? How is she? When is she coming to see me?"

Her mother hesitated. "I haven't seen her to talk to," she said finally. "But she seems—fine."

Maribeth heard the little catch in her mother's voice. "There's something you're not telling me."

Her mother fingered one corner of the bedsheet. "It's just—I don't think you should get your hopes up about Christine coming to see you."

Maribeth stared at her. "What? Of course she'll come to see me—she's my best friend!"

"The accident was—hard on her." Her mother didn't meet her eyes. "She's—changed."

"Changed? How?"

"I shouldn't say anything. Maybe I'm wrong. Maybe she will come to see you. Maybe, now that you're all right, she'll straighten out."

"Straighten out? What do you mean, straighten out?"

But her mother wouldn't say anything more, and must have warned Maribeth's father, too, because Maribeth got no more satisfaction from him the next time he came to see her; and Dr. Ryback said what Christine did after leaving the hospital was none of her business. However, she did point out to Maribeth that neither Christine nor any other non-family members would be permitted to visit her while she was in intensive care. "The hospital administrator is very strict about rules like that," she said.

With that Maribeth had to be content—but wasn't.

The night before she was to go home, a week after awakening, she dreamed.

In her dream she woke to find the hospital room filled with flames: those on her left green and hissing, those on her right red and roaring. At first that was all she could see, but gradually something dark took shape within each fire, coming slowly into focus, until, horrified, she saw a person trapped in the flames to either side. Somehow she knew she could rescue them, if only she could move, but though she hadn't been strapped to the bed since that first day, in her dream the straps were back, and the more she struggled the tighter they became, while the two tortured figures writhed in agony and then began to scream...

She jerked upright in bed, gasping, the screams—or her scream?—still echoing in her head. No monitor recorded her heartbeat any longer, but she didn't need one to know that her pulse was racing.

She wiped sweat from her forehead with the sleeve of her hospital gown. *Where had such a nightmare come from?* She lay back, and slowly stopped trembling. *Green fire? People burning to death? Horrible....*

The gray fog of returning sleep swallowed her last conscious thought, *You never asked how Tom died....*

Dr. Ryback and all the nurses who had looked after Maribeth during her two-month nap came down to the lobby to see her off the next day. "It won't be the same without you," Dr. Ryback told her with a grin. "You'd become very popular with the interns, you know. They used to wonder if any of them were enough like Prince Charming to wake you with a kiss."

Maribeth blushed, then laughed. "Tell them it probably would have turned them into frogs, instead."

The head nurse came forward with a bouquet of flowers "for being the quietest patient on the wing for the last two months." Maribeth shook hands with her, then with the rest of the nurses, and then with Dr. Ryback again. Her father followed suit, telling the doctor, "I can't tell you how much it means to us to have her back. How can we thank you?"

Dr. Ryback shook her head. "I'd love to take the credit. But whatever brought her back happened somewhere inside herself."

Maribeth's father looked at her appraisingly, and she grinned. "Beats me," she said. "But I'm sure glad it did."

"We all are." Her mother gave her a hug. "Now, is your coat zipped up tight?"

Maribeth sighed. "Yes, Mom."

"Then let's go. Come on, John. Let Dr. Ryback get back to her rounds."

"Good-bye!" Maribeth called to the doctor as she followed her parents out.

Dr. Ryback, already in the elevator, waved as the doors slid shut.

Outside the air sparkled with ice crystals, and sun-dogs made twin spots of cold light on either side of the sun, low in the southeast. Maribeth stopped suddenly in the parking lot as her parents led the way to their blue Chrysler four-door, and stared around with a strange sense of distorted déjà vu.

The hospital topped the only sizeable hill within twenty miles. To her right, south, the prairie stretched endlessly, treeless and brown, for despite the cold, little snow had fallen yet. To her left houses and industrial areas sprawled around the slightly taller buildings—and ubiquitous grain elevators—of Weyburn's downtown core. Winding through the city, and curling around the base of the hill, was the Souris River.

Maribeth had lived in Weyburn all her life. She had been to General Hospital many times to visit friends or for this or that minor emergency or test. She had seen this view more times than she could count.

So why had it seemed to her, for a moment, that there should be trees, not barren fields, stretching to the horizon, and that the city shouldn't be there at all?

Her mother looked back at her. "Maribeth, are you all right?"

She shook herself mentally and nodded. "I'm fine. I was just...enjoying the view. It's been a long time since I've been out, remember?"

"We're not likely to forget," said her father drily. "Now get in. It's been a long time since you've been home, too, you know."

Yes, it had, Maribeth thought as they drove down the hill and across town. In fact, it had been a long time since she had been anywhere. She craned her neck to see Weyburn Comprehensive School, just a block away as they turned north off Government Road onto First Avenue. She was eager to get back and see her friends—especially Christine, especially after what her mother had said—but at the same time the thought was kind of scary. *What would they think? How would they treat her?* "I'll slug anybody that calls me Sleeping Beauty," she muttered.

"What, dear?" her mother asked.

She started. "Nothing! Just thinking about going back to school."

"Well, that's still three weeks away, after Christmas. You just think about getting all your strength back before then."

Christmas! Maribeth had almost forgotten about that. "This is December 19, isn't it?"

"Mmmm-hmmm."

"Not much time left for me to shop."

"Don't even think about it," her mother said. "You're to stay home for another two weeks. Doctor's orders."

"I don't remember Dr. Ryback—"

"I do," her mother replied, and that was that.

Maribeth decided the doctor and her mother were right when she climbed out of the car in the driveway of their two-story white-brick house and felt her knees tremble. Besides, she'd always hated Christmas shopping.

When her father pushed open the front door, Maribeth was almost knocked over by a small sand-colored bundle of fur and furious sound. "Down, Miser, down!" ordered her father, but the ecstatic cocker spaniel ignored him.

Maribeth laughed. "It's all right, Dad." She dropped to one knee to fondle the dog's ears and got her face licked frantically in return. "I'm glad he missed me."

"Even I missed you, M.B.," said a new voice, and Maribeth looked up to see Sean, his hands in his pockets, giving her an awkward twelve-year-old's grin from the corner of the banister.

"I missed you, too, punk." She got up and hugged him. His face turned red but he kept his grin.

"You get settled back in your room and I'll start dinner," said her mother, and her father, carrying her small suitcase, led the way upstairs.

He walked straight into her room and set down the luggage, but she stopped in the doorway, feeling another twinge of—it was almost like double vision. Of course her room should be blue-and-white, with rock-star posters decorating one wall and a vast display of friends' school pictures covering the bulletin board over the computer desk.

Then why had she been expecting to see a stone cell with two low-slung cots and little else?

"There you are," her father said. "Just the way you left it..." His voice broke a little, and he gave her a crooked grin very much like Sean's. "Welcome home." He hugged her

68

tightly, then kissed the top of her head and went out, calling over his shoulder, "Dinner in half an hour."

Maribeth turned to the suitcase, intending to unpack, but as she did so the largest picture on the bulletin board caught her eye. It showed a slender girl with dark eyes, long, shiny black hair, and a sardonic twist to her smile. Scrawled across one corner in black felt pen was, "Your friend to the end, Christine."

On impulse, Maribeth reached for the telephone.

The number came easily to her mind—how many hundreds of times had she dialed it in the eight or nine years she and Christine had been best friends? After two rings, someone said, "Hello?"

Maribeth's heart jumped. "Christine?"

A pause. "Who is this?"

Maribeth's face split in an uncontrollable grin. "Sleeping Beauty!"

"What?"

"Maribeth, dummy! Maribeth! You know, your best friend? I know I haven't been around for a while, but—"

"Maribeth?" Christine's voice was strangely flat. "Oh, yeah. I remember."

"What do you mean, you remember?" Maribeth's grin faded. "How could you forget?"

"I didn't forget. I just hadn't thought about you recently."

"What?"

"Look, I've got to go. I've got things to do."

"Christine—"

The line went dead, leaving Maribeth holding the useless receiver—and feeling as if she'd been clubbed with it.

9

Christmas...and Christine

Maribeth only played with her food at dinner, chasing one pea around and around the plate with her fork until her father finally said, a hint of exasperation in his voice, "Maribeth, either eat that pea or put it out of its misery. Don't torture it."

She looked up, startled. "What?"

"You really should eat," her mother chimed in. "You've still got to build up your strength."

"First time you ever had to tell her to eat!" Sean said, grinning.

Maribeth ignored him. "I'm sorry," she said. "I'm just—not hungry."

Her mother leaned forward, and Maribeth saw that her knuckles had gone white on the hand that held her fork. "You're not feeling bad, are you?"

"No, Mom, no, nothing like that," Maribeth assured her hastily. She was beginning to understand a little better how worried her parents had been for the past two months, and how worried they still must be.

"Then why—?"

"It's Christine."

Her parents exchanged glances, but said nothing. Sean, however, had no compunction. "Boy, oh boy, sis, she's really gone nutzoid since your smash-up," he crowed. "I

70

mean, she was always a little strange, even stranger than you, but now—"

"Sean," said his father, and his tone was such that the boy broke off, stared at his father with his mouth open for a moment, then quickly resumed shovelling in his food.

"What does he mean?" Maribeth demanded. "Nutzoid?"

"Sean, leave the table, please," her mother said.

"But I haven't had dessert—"

"Dessert will wait. We'll call you."

Sean, grumbling, took his glass of Pepsi and stalked out of the kitchen. Maribeth looked from parent to parent. "Mom? Dad?"

"Christine has changed since the accident," her father said. "Your brother is quite right. Even before that she was getting a little wild—"

Maribeth had a brief flash of memory from the night of the crash, with Christine in the front seat nuzzling Tom's neck and urging him to drive faster and faster... "It's just her family situation," she said uncomfortably. "Ever since the divorce..."

"No," her mother said, suddenly fierce. "It's more than that. I think she's on drugs."

"Christine would never—"

"She was drunk the night of the accident. So was Tom. The coroner's inquest established that."

"Well, sure, she drinks a little. Most of the kids in school do. But she'd never do drugs—"

"Some other time we can argue about the difference," her father said drily. "You're right, we're not sure about the drugs—"

"I'm sure," her mother interjected.

"—but the point is, Christine has changed. She's changed her looks, her way of dressing, her way of

71

talking—and she's hanging out with a very bad crowd. As bad as they come."

"What do you mean? Who?"

"A gang."

"A gang? But that's ridiculous. There aren't any gangs in Weyburn. It's too small."

"There weren't any two months ago. There's one now."

"And Christine doesn't just 'hang out' with the Ice Devils," Maribeth's mother said. "She runs them. I think she started them."

Maribeth felt dizzy. This was all impossible; none of it matched her two-month-old memories of Christine. But the fact remained she had telephoned her old friend, and her "old friend" had cut her off cold.

Her father covered her hand with his big, strong one. "I'm sorry. I know it's hard for you to hear these things. That's why we didn't want to talk to you about Christine. We hoped it could wait until just before you went back to school."

"I just wanted to talk to her," Maribeth whispered. "It's been two months—and we were in the accident together—and Tom...but she hung up on me. She wasn't even interested. It was like—like I was dead, too!"

"It's more like she is." Her mother came around the table and put her arm around Maribeth's shoulders. "But you're still here. And you haven't changed—she has. You'll find other friends."

Maribeth nodded, but in her heart she wondered if she wanted new friends. *It hurts too much to have them,* she thought, and the words seemed to echo in her mind with peculiar force.

Sean poked his head back into the kitchen and surveyed the tableau. "If you three have finished, I'd like my dessert now."

72

Maribeth squeezed her father's hand and gave her mother a hug, then said to Sean, "Look who's talking about never having to be told to eat!" and started clearing the table, finding the clatter of knives and forks and plates somehow comforting.

As the Christmas holidays passed, Maribeth regained her strength and worried less and less about the occasional moments of oddness. Usually they came when she saw something for the first time since her accident. The television made her pulse race when she walked into the living room and saw its moving picture; she felt an unreasoning urge to back out and run. But the sensation passed so quickly that ten minutes later she watched Star Trek with impunity.

There was a similar incident with the stereo, augmented by the strange fact that although her memories told her a group called Hard-Boiled Steel was her favorite band, she found she couldn't stand their latest album. In fact, all music sounded strange to her.

Christmas, however, was an unexpected joy. She had memories of several special Christmases, but somehow this was the best of all. The tall Scotch pine in the living room was the most beautiful thing she had ever seen. Holly and mistletoe and carols and eggnog—it all seemed fresh and exciting, as it hadn't for years.

Her parents toasted her recovery at Christmas dinner, with Dr. Ryback as guest of honor. "To the best Christmas ever," her father said, his eyes meeting Maribeth's over his glass and his familiar crooked smile wrinkling his face. "Courtesy of Dr. Ryback."

Dr. Ryback laughed and sipped from her glass, then said, "I told you, Mr. Gayle—"

"John, please."

"John, then. I told you, I really don't think I had anything to do with it."

"We've already thanked God," Maribeth's father said reasonably. "You're next in line. Take what you can get. For example, take some of this turkey—" He piled several slices on a plate and passed it to her.

"Thank you." Dr. Ryback reached for the dressing.

Maribeth accepted her own helping of turkey. "If there was nothing physically wrong with me, why did I stay unconscious so long?"

"If I knew that, I'd just accept my Nobel Prize and retire," the doctor said ruefully. "The brain is incredibly complex, and we're only beginning to understand some of its most basic principles. One theory in cases like yours is that the mind—the mind, as opposed to the brain—has been traumatized. It retreats from reality into itself. Then, when it feels ready to deal with the trauma, either directly or by purging it from its memories, it surfaces, and the patient wakes. Pass the cranberry sauce, please."

Maribeth obliged. "I can't remember anything about the accident," she said slowly.

"It's only a general theory," the doctor said. "It might not apply in your case—but then again, it might. Your friend—"

"Doctor, it's Christmas," Maribeth's father warned. "I think we should change the subject."

"But, Dad, I'd like to know!" Maribeth objected.

Her father looked at her, hesitated, then said, "All right. But if you start torturing peas again, that's it."

Maribeth laughed, and so did Dr. Ryback, in the self-conscious manner of one who doesn't really get the joke.

"So you think seeing Tom—die—" Maribeth went on.

"—could have been enough trauma to drive your consciousness underground, so to speak," the doctor said. "Two months later, your mind had buried the unpleasantness, and you woke up. Simple as that."

What about the dreams? Maribeth thought, but she said nothing. If there were nothing wrong with her brain, then any problems she was having had to be in her mind, and there was no way she was going to a psychologist. She'd have enough trouble at school as Sleeping Beauty without becoming the designated psycho, too. "More dressing, doctor?"

Throughout the holidays, Maribeth kept hoping Christine would call, or come by, or at least acknowledge her existence. But she heard nothing, and after her earlier rebuff, she couldn't bring herself to dial the familiar number again. Instead she ate, slept, read, watched TV, fought with her brother (normal relations having resumed shortly after the "gee-I'm-glad-you're-home" stage), and tried to get used to the way her parents, especially her mother, watched her every move as though afraid she would break.

At first it annoyed her, but her mother was obviously trying so hard not to, while at the same time being unable to stop hovering, that it touched her. She wondered why it seemed strange to her to discover how much her parents loved her. Hadn't she always known it?

Maybe it took something like this to prove it to me, she thought. There's a big difference between knowing and feeling.

Finally the holidays wound down, the house decorations were packed away, and the tree was put in the back yard to shed its needles all over the snow. The needles, which began shedding just three days before Christmas, now lay thick over everything. The night before returning to school, Maribeth lay sleepless in her bed, listening to the rising howl of a bitter northwest wind, thinking about Christine. *Tomorrow I'll see her,* she thought. *And she'll see me. Surely she won't brush me off again. We've been friends so long...*

Her bedroom door opened a crack, and a beam of yellow light from the hallway struck her eyes. Her mother pushed the door open a little further. "Maribeth? Honey, why aren't you asleep?"

Maribeth said nothing.

"You're thinking about Christine, aren't you?"

To her alarm, Maribeth's lower lip trembled. Her mother came in and sat on the side of her bed. Her cool fingers brushed back Maribeth's hair. "It's hard to lose a friend, isn't it?"

"But she's not lost," Maribeth whispered. "That's what's so hard. She's right where she's always been—but she's not interested in me any more. And we've been friends for—for so long—" She swallowed a growing lump in her throat.

"I know you have, dear," her mother murmured. "But you're both growing up, and you've both been through something terrible. You've reacted differently. Remember what Dr. Ryback said? Your mind put you to sleep until it was ready to deal with it, and then you woke up. Maybe Christine never has figured out how to deal with it. Maybe—maybe when she does, she'll be your friend again." But her voice lacked conviction.

Maribeth struggled upright. "You don't really want that to happen, do you? You don't want me to have anything to do with Christine ever again! Has she really turned that bad? Mom, even if she's on drugs, she could still turn around—"

"It's not that." Her mother picked at the handmade quilt covering the bed. "I just—I don't want her around you, that's all."

76

"But why? She's my friend—I have to try to help her. If the accident is what made her change, I have to try even harder. No one else went through it except me—"

"That's just it." Her mother's voice turned hard. "You weren't the one drinking. There wasn't any alcohol in your blood. But you were the one who was almost killed. You were almost killed, and it was Christine's fault. That's why I don't want you to have anything more to do with her. What she's doing now is just as dangerous as drinking in a car. She's going to get herself or someone else hurt, and this time I don't want it to be you!" She stopped and took a deep breath. "I'm sorry. It's just—I love you so much, and when I thought you might—die—"

Maribeth touched her hand. "I promise I won't do anything as stupid as riding with someone who's been drinking again, Mom. And you know I won't take any drugs, if that's what Christine's involved with. But if there's anything I can do to help her—I have to try. I love you—but I love her, too. Not as much, or the same way—but I do."

Her mother sat very still for a moment, then nodded, leaned forward and kissed Maribeth's forehead. "I know you do. But please—be careful tomorrow."

Maribeth forced a laugh as her mother stood up. "I'm just going to school, Mom. What could happen?"

Her mother didn't reply. The door closed silently behind her.

10

The Ice Devils

Maribeth woke early, couldn't get back to sleep despite the winter morning darkness, and was dressed and brushing her hair for the third time when her father knocked on her door. She surprised her mother by being downstairs before the table was even set for breakfast. "First time you ever came on the first call," her father noted as he broke eggs into a frying pan.

"I guess I'm just—anxious," Maribeth replied. She had been going to say "scared," but, remembering how she had reassured her mother that nothing could happen to her at school, changed her mind in mid-sentence. "I'm two months behind, and the semester is over in another three weeks. How can I ever catch up?"

"Well, we won't count on straight A's," said her mother, setting a plate of toast on the table.

Maribeth took a slice and began buttering it. "But what if I don't even pass?"

"Then you'll make it up in summer school," her father said. "No problem. You inherited your father's brains, you know."

Her mother gave him a withering look. "And his modesty?"

Maribeth laughed.

Still, it was with a fluttery feeling in her stomach that she walked the four blocks to the Comprehensive in the red light of the rising sun. As she passed the third house down the street, deep, throat-tearing barking erupted from behind the high chain-link fence surrounding the yard. She flinched, caught herself, and glared through the mesh. A massive pit bull terrier, chained to a stake by the front door, glared at her with unreasoning hostility in its round black eyes. "Shut up, Brutus," she said, but the dog redoubled its attempts to get at her, and with a shiver she hurried on. Brutus's barking didn't normally scare her, but today... She ran down her list of worries in her mind: coming back to school after missing weeks and weeks; whispers behind her back in the hall; sideways glances; strange dreams and stranger daydreams—and meeting Christine again. For some reason that scared her most of all.

The meeting came a lot sooner than she expected.

The Comprehensive was really two buildings joined together, an older structure of red brick, built before the First World War, and a twenty-year-old modern addition of gray cement and stucco, low and spread out over three times the area of the original school. The main entrance opened onto a street already lined with student cars. Parked closest were three older-model Firebirds, one black, one red and one gray, all with oversize tires, mag wheels and chrome exhausts.

Lounging on the hoods and trunks of the cars were half a dozen boys wearing tight blue jeans, black motocross boots and unzipped black leather jackets over red ski vests. Maribeth stared at them as she approached. Last night's wind had sent the mercury plunging, but the boys acted as if it were the middle of July.

They spoke in low voices, ignoring everyone else, including Maribeth; but as she reached the curb across from them, they straightened as if coming to attention, and looked at the King Street corner.

Automatically Maribeth followed their gaze, and saw a gleaming white, brand-new Camaro round the curb, fishtailing slightly on the ice, and roll toward the row of old Firebirds and the space left between the first two. Since the Camaro's parallel parking maneuver occurred directly over the crosswalk, Maribeth waited until it was done, then started across the street.

As she crossed the center line the door of the Camaro opened and Christine got out.

Maribeth stopped dead, hardly able to believe the leather-and-zipper-bedecked, wild-haired girl who emerged from the car was her best friend. Christine barely glanced at her, turning instead toward the boys who were congregating around her, then stiffened and turned back, like a hound catching a threatening scent. Maribeth's uncertain smile died in the cold hostility of Christine's gaze. "Look, Ice Devils," she said. "It's Sleeping Beauty."

The boys turned as one to look at Maribeth, their eyes filled with the same unreasoning meanness as the pit bull's. "Did Prince Charming kiss you awake?" taunted one.

"I'll bet it took more than a kiss," said another.

"I'll bet I could have woken her up," said a third.

"Maybe you'll get another chance."

"Maybe she'll fall asleep again."

"Hey, Sleeping Beauty, you fall asleep again, we'll all come wake you up."

"Yeah, you feel drowsy, you just call the Ice Devils."

One of the older boys took a step toward her. "I think she looks a little sleepy right now."

Another stepped forward. "Maybe we should help her out."

One opened the door of the lead Firebird. "Come on, Sleeping Beauty, we'll make sure you stay awake in class."

Maribeth edged back, staring wide-eyed and horrified at Christine, who leaned on the Camaro, idly examining her long nails.

One of the Devils made clucking sounds, like he was calling a puppy. "Come on, Beauty, come to Prince Charming."

"Christine!" The plea burst out of Maribeth as she backed off another step, on the verge of running, unable to believe her friend would just stand there and do nothing to help her.

"Maribeth." Christine looked up from her nails. "You should have stayed in the hospital, Maribeth. You should have stayed asleep. You would have been better off. A whole lot better off." She straightened suddenly. "Come on, Devils." She strode toward the school, trailed by the gang, but stopped on the sidewalk and, copied by all the boys, looked back at Maribeth, still standing in the road. "Bye-bye, Sleeping Beauty. See you later."

Maribeth stayed rooted where she was, staring after them. *One word,* she thought. *It only took her one word to turn them all against me. She runs this gang!*

The honk of an oncoming car broke her reverie. She hurried across the street, avoiding the Firebirds, then started running as the bell rang.

Inside there was no sign of Christine or the Ice Devils, most of whom Maribeth knew by reputation, if not by name. They were the worst troublemakers in school, but they'd never been organized into a gang before. Christine had done that. Why?

Maribeth frowned as she hurried through the echoing hallways, deserted except for one or two latecomers like herself. One of the Devils—the first one to speak—seemed more familiar to her than the others. Very familiar. "Rick," she said out loud. "Rick Trudgeon." That was his name, but how did she know it? When she reached into her memory, there was nothing but an image of his face, the sound of his name—and a strange uneasiness.

Morning classes provided more than enough distraction to keep any missing memories submerged. The two months she had missed proved just as problematic as she had feared, especially in algebra and chemistry. There was no particular difficulty in English, except she knew the class had covered the entire script of Macbeth while she was in hospital.

One thing, however, worked out better than she had hoped. Her classmates welcomed her back warmly, after a few hesitant first advances, and soon she felt as if she had never left. At lunchtime she headed for the cafeteria with two other girls, Ellen Hodgkiss and Crystal Copeland, her best-friends-besides-Christine, who were comparing notes on some new boy in school Maribeth hadn't seen yet.

"He's the best-looking senior," said Ellen.

"He's the best-looking boy, period," said Crystal.

"That's not saying much, in this school!" Ellen retorted, and they laughed.

"Who are you talking about?" Maribeth asked.

Ellen gave her a wide-eyed look. "Where have you been?" she demanded incredulously, and Maribeth took a swipe at her with her algebra book.

"Adam Metcalfe." Crystal rolled her eyes. "He just moved here over Christmas from Vancouver. He's so sexy!" A boy from their class, going the other way, bumped into her and she turned to shout after him, "Watch where you're going, crapface!"

"It's just because he's new," Maribeth said. "I'll bet he's no sexier than—than Harold Coffey."

"Give me a break!" Ellen cried, and Crystal made gagging noises.

They were still giggling when they entered the cafeteria—and the Ice Devils blocked their way.

Maribeth saw Rick leering at her, but only Christine spoke. "So how are you enjoying your first day back in school, Sleeping Beauty?" she said in a sing-song voice, making the harmless question sound like a threat.

"Leave her alone, Christine!" Ellen said. "You know what the principal said—"

"You think I care?" Christine smiled sweetly. "So what if he suspends me? I've got better things to do. We all do, don't we, Devils?"

The boys around her nodded, except for Rick, who kept his gaze locked on Maribeth. She stared back at him for a minute, trying to dredge up the elusive memory, but only succeeded in strengthening her uneasiness. She looked away from him, back at Christine. "Let us through, Christine. We're hungry."

"Why, after all that beddy-bye time, I'll just bet you are. Don't let us stop you. We were just leaving. We just wanted to tell you, Sleeping Beauty, that we'll see you after school. Have a nice day." The gang went out, Rick the last to leave and the only one to look back.

Ellen turned wide eyes on Maribeth. "What are you going to do?"

"They're just trying to scare me," Maribeth said with more confidence than she felt. "They won't do anything."

"Don't be so sure," said Crystal. "They're getting worse and worse. I heard they beat up little Marvin Rhodes so bad he could hardly walk." She lowered her voice. "And you know what everyone's saying about Winona Manson..."

"Since when do you believe what 'everyone's saying'?" Maribeth said loudly. "Come on, are we here to talk or eat?"

They joined the short line, pushing their brown plastic trays down the metal rails. Bored-looking women in stained white aprons dumped fried chicken, green beans and mashed potatoes on their plates at one end of the line and shoved slices of burned apple pie at them at the other. Maribeth made a face. "I think I'll go back on intravenous," she said, but her friends barely smiled.

"I don't understand why Christine has it in for you," Ellen said as they took seats at one of the long tables. "She's your best friend."

Maribeth shrugged uncomfortably.

"Is it because of the accident?" asked Crystal. "Is that why she..." her voice trailed off, but Maribeth could fill in the blanks.

"Hates me? I don't know. I don't remember the accident."

"Well, Christine hasn't been the same since. At first she was just kind of out of it, like she was here, but she wasn't really *here*, you know? But then suddenly she turned nasty, and the next thing we knew, she had that bunch of losers calling themselves the Ice Devils. I mean, you'd think this was New York, or something. Who ever heard of a gang in Weyburn, Saskatchewan?"

"So what are you going to do?" Ellen asked Maribeth again.

"About what?"

"About Christine! About 'after school!'"

"Maybe she just wants to talk?"

"Right," said Ellen. "Talk."

"Sure," said Crystal. "Talk."

They sat silently for a moment, then Maribeth sighed and pushed her plate away. "Anybody want my chicken?"

84

11

After School

Maribeth and Christine were supposed to share two classes in the afternoon, social studies and cosmetology, but Christine was absent from both, a fact the teacher in each instance noted with something approaching relief—relief Maribeth shared, then felt guilty for. Christine, whatever had happened to her, had been her friend. Somewhere under that harsh new look and strange behavior, she still was her friend. She had to be, with the memories they shared. She had to be!

But how to get through to that friend? Maribeth pondered as she gave one of her cosmetology classmates a penetrating hair treatment. Her fingers kneaded the other girl's short blonde hair—hair that would have been long and glossy black, had everything been as it should be. She and Christine had always used each other for partners in cosmetology.

She stared out the window at the far end of the long line of chairs and sinks and plastic-aproned hairwashers and washees. The sky was slate gray and slowly sifting a fine, powdery snow onto the city, and for a moment it seemed the only familiar, unchanged thing in Maribeth's life. The sky had looked just like that the day of the accident....

Someone called her. "Hey. Hey!" She blinked and looked down at the girl with her head in the sink. "Where'd you go? Your hands quit moving."

"Sorry." Maribeth quickly finished up and reached for the rinse hose. "Daydreaming, I guess." The other girl muttered something. "What was that?"

"Nothing."

Maribeth was pretty sure the girl had actually said, "I'd have thought you'd had enough dreaming," but she resisted the temptation to make the rinse ice cold. She *had* been dawdling.

Biology rounded out the school day, and once again Maribeth was reminded of how far behind she had fallen. Her concentration on the differing actions of organic enzymes and inorganic solvents on slivers of raw liver was not helped by the realization that whatever Christine had planned for "after school" was only minutes away.

The bell rang. Maribeth gathered up her books and made for her locker, accompanied by the oddly silent Ellen and Crystal, who exchanged worried glances when they thought she wasn't looking. Maribeth wished she had someone to exchange worried glances with, too, but she wouldn't let her friends know her heart was pounding and her palms tingling with sweat. She did her best to look serenely unconcerned.

She expected Christine and the Ice Devils to be waiting by their cars out front. But once again they surprised her.

They were waiting by her locker.

She, Ellen and Crystal stopped as they rounded the corner into the short hallway which contained their lockers. The Devils, leaning against the blue metal doors, were ranged on either side of the hall, with Christine at the far end, her back to a fire exit, watching. Maribeth stared at her former friend, who stared back with a blank, closed look that chilled her—and then terrified her, because just for an instant, Christine seemed to glow—as though a dark, blood-red fire burned beneath her skin. The image came and went within a fraction of a second, but Maribeth knew she had seen it—she could see it still in her mind's eye.

Her pulse raced faster. Am I going crazy? she wondered.

"What do we do?" Ellen whispered behind her, and for a moment Maribeth thought she had seen that strange vision, too. But that was impossible.

Just as it was impossible she had seen it.

"Run," said Crystal.

Maribeth stiffened her back and her resolve. "You do what you like. I'm going to my locker." And with that she strode down the hallway, though her heart fluttered like a bird trapped beneath her breastbone.

Rick Trudgeon leaned against her locker. "You want something, Sleeping Beauty?"

"I want into my locker. Please move."

"Oh, of course!" Rick stepped aside and made an elaborate, mocking bow. "Be my guest!"

Maribeth licked dry lips and took the lock in her hand, holding her books under her arm. It took her three attempts to successfully dial the combination, but at last the lock popped open and she lifted the handle of the locker. She'd barely started to pull the door open when Rick snatched at it and banged it wide open. Maribeth's books crashed to the floor. "So what have you got in here, Beauty?" He stepped up close behind her, pinning her against the locker, looking over her head into the interior. "You got a picture of me?"

"No," she gasped. "Please, you're squashing me..."

"I'm squashing you?" Rick's voice dropped to a whisper and his lips touched her ear. "No, baby, I'm squeezing you. You like being squeezed, don't you? Especially by me."

"I don't—"

"Don't remember? Don't remember?" Rick grabbed her shoulder and spun her around, then pushed her back against the locker and straddled her, his right hand cupping her chin. "Think, babe. Think really hard. Think back to August. That old farm. Midnight. Think back to my Firebird. That's why I was so hurt when you wouldn't get in this morning, Sleeping Beauty. You got in readily enough back then."

And suddenly Maribeth did remember. She had gone to a party with Christine, and for the first and only time let Christine talk her into drinking. The party had gotten wilder and wilder, and next thing she knew she was driving out into the country with Rick. And then...

"You do remember, don't you, babe?" Rick's breath burned in her ear. "You chickened out on me. We were going places, Beauty. You and me. We were on our way. But you cut and run. I told you then that some day I was going to finish what we started. So now we're going to go outside, you and me and all the Devils, and you're going to get in my Firebird again, and then we're going to go someplace real quiet and make up for August. 'Cause you're mine, Sleeping Beauty. You're all mine. Christine says so."

Maribeth twisted her head to the left and saw Christine still standing at the end of the hall, smiling in a way that drove a dagger into Maribeth's heart—a smile that vanished as a big hand suddenly grabbed Rick's shoulder and pulled him off Maribeth.

The hallway rattled as the Devils straightened from their posts on the locker doors. Maribeth's rescuer, a tall, muscular boy in a gray sweatsuit, glared at them. "Come on, punks! One at a time or all at once, I don't care."

Rick lunged at him, but pulled up almost comically short as Christine said, "No." He whirled toward her, but she met his glare coolly. "Not here."

Flushed, Rick spun back toward the tall boy and thrust a finger under his nose. "Later!" he growled.

"Any time, creep!"

Rick's fists clenched and Maribeth thought he would ignore Christine's order and start swinging, but Ellen and Crystal returned at that moment with a puffing, overweight man in an ugly blue suit, who blustered into the hallway with all the authority he could muster. "Break it up, break it up! You kids clear out of here!"

The Devils all glanced at Christine, who nodded. As one they turned and marched out, banging each locker with their fists as they passed, ignoring the man in the blue suit, who stayed well clear of them.

As Christine passed, Maribeth grabbed her arm. "Christine—" But she let go and fell back, gasping, seeing again, for the barest instant, Christine's body filled with flame.

Christine paused. "You're not Rick's anymore," she said in a whisper that crawled down Maribeth's spine like an ice-cold worm. "You're mine." And then she stalked away, disdainful of all of them: the tall boy, the man in the blue suit, Ellen and Crystal—and especially Maribeth.

"What was that all about?" asked the man. Maribeth finally recognized him as the vice-principal. But she couldn't answer his question; hardly even heard it. Her mind whirled. She was going crazy—she had to be. Hallucinations. And her memory—how could she have forgotten Rick...?

The thought of her and Rick together filled her with horror, a different kind of horror than she had felt at her strange vision of Christine. The thought of being with any boy, at that moment, was terrifying. Yet she could remember many dates now, dates that had somehow been obliterated from her mind until Rick reminded her of that horrible moment in his car...what was wrong with her?

"Are you all right?" someone asked her. She blinked, and finally focused on the boy who had pulled Rick away, who was looking at her with concern.

"No..." she whispered, and then, when he reached out to touch her, screamed, "Leave me alone!" ducked under his arm and ran, down the hallway, out into the cold air, coatless and gloveless, and across the schoolyard toward the street that led to home and sanity.

Down at the corner of King Street tires squealed as the last of the Ice Devils' Firebirds accelerated away, its rumbling exhaust echoing from the high walls of the old part of the school like mocking laughter.

12

Adam

Maribeth's parents weren't home when she barged through the front door. She closed it and leaned back against it, her bare arms wrapped around her body, shivering as much from reaction as from the cold. Her father, she knew, would still be at the jewelry store he managed; her mother at her recently acquired job as secretary to the local provincial court judge, which she had taken during Maribeth's two-month absence, and which had surprised Maribeth when she found out. Though she knew her mother had worked before she was born, all Maribeth's life she had been one of those housewives who some people said didn't exist any more, and had always, always been home when Maribeth returned from school.

But now she wasn't, and Maribeth, hearing the emptiness of the big house, sank down and folded her arms over her pulled-up knees. Burying her face, she felt more alone than she had ever felt in her life...

...and for a moment she felt that wasn't true, that she had felt far lonelier many times before...

...and she jerked her head up wildly. Again! She forgot things she should never have forgotten, remembered things that had never happened. Dr. Ryback's tests had said there was nothing wrong with her, but something had to be messed up in her head—how else to explain what was happening?

She pulled herself upright, using as a crutch the little black table with the skinny white vase on it that had stood by the door for as long as she could remember. Over it hung a hexagonal mirror in a gold frame, and she looked into it and into her own eyes, dark and haunted-looking. "You look," she told her image, "as bad as I feel."

She stood there for a long time, staring at herself, feeling that something was about to happen. But nothing did. Her image didn't crack like the ice on November puddles, or burst into blood-colored flame like Christine's had. She didn't suddenly remember another disastrous date, or have some bizarre recollection of flying over a pink jungle on a purple dragon. In fact, the more she looked at herself, the more normal she appeared, until finally she found herself worrying more about her smudged make-up than the state of her mind, and that brought a tentative smile to her lips. She leaned her forehead against the cool smoothness of the mirror and took a deep breath, feeling calmer.

The door crashed open and two snowy figures burst into the hallway, one on four legs, the other on two, both yelling at the top of their voices and bringing with them a great wave of cold air and a miniature blizzard as they shook themselves.

"Sean!" Maribeth cried, exasperated, stepping out of the sudden flurry. "Miser! You look like you've been rolling in the snow!"

"We have!" said her snowsuited younger brother, pulling his red toque off his tousled head and grinning at her, while Miser answered by trying to leap up high enough to lick her face, and came close to succeeding.

"Down, boy, down!" Maribeth commanded, then added to her brother, "Well, you'd better get this hallway cleaned up before Mom and Dad get home—and keep this mutt—" she knelt and ruffled Miser's ears, which made him almost shake himself to pieces with ecstasy, "—off the furniture and the living room carpet until he's dried out, or you'll both end up in hot water, and I don't mean a bath."

"Aw, Maree-Beth, loosen up!" Sean grabbed Miser. "Look, I've got him, right? Now will you hold him while I get out of my environmental protection unit?"

"If you mean your snowsuit—" Maribeth took the dog's collar. "I guess so."

Miser barked and managed to lick her face after all.

By the time Sean was finally installed in front of the TV, and Miser was clean and dry enough to be allow into the kitchen to eat, Maribeth had managed to convince herself that she wasn't as crazy as she had thought. How could anything be seriously wrong when she was standing on the familiar red-and-white linoleum of the kitchen, scraping dog food into Miser's bowl, while rap music blasted in the other room?

There's no reason to bother Mom and Dad—they've had to worry about me long enough, she told herself firmly, hearing the family Chrysler roll up and stop outside with a familiar squeal of brakes. *I just overreacted to finding out how much Christine's changed. Sure, it was a shock, but I can handle it. I'll just avoid her. If she doesn't want to be friends any more, well, I can live with that. I've got other friends.*

She thought suddenly of the boy who had pulled Rick away from her. She didn't even know his name, and she'd been awfully rude to him. She flushed a little, remembering. *Tomorrow,* she told herself, *I'll find out who he is and apologize.*

Then the back door opened, and she turned to her father with a smile, as her mother's car also pulled up outside. "Hi, pumpkin," said her dad. "How was your first day back at school?"

"Fine," she said. "Just fine."

♌ ♌ ♌ ♌ ♌

The woman's voice was familiar, and comforting. "To some it looks like a fire shining through the skin, as though they're burning from the inside out..."

The voice faded, and Christine's face loomed out of the vague darkness, burning, burning, engulfed in blood-red flames, her eyes filled with hatred...

From somewhere behind Maribeth came the voice of a boy, a boy in agony, whispering, "Help me, help me, please help me, oh God, someone help me, it hurts, God it hurts..."

And then Christine reached out a flaming hand and touched a shining puddle on the ground and everything around Maribeth exploded into fire and the boy's voice rose in a scream...

And Maribeth woke, gasping, drenched in sweat, the dream already fading. In a moment its horror was only a vague memory, like the woman's voice, so tantalizingly familiar, saying...saying...what?

But it was gone, and with it the fear, and as her heart slowed Maribeth fell back into sleep.

In the morning she remembered none of it.

♌ ♌ ♌ ♌ ♌

Maribeth left for school refreshed and confident—and wearing a coat that was much too light for the bitter cold, which had intensified overnight. She timed her departure carefully to coincide with the greatest amount of confusion, so that no one would ask her where her regular winter coat was, and got away with it; but halfway to school, the snow crunching beneath her feet and her breath coming in great frosty clouds, she wished her mother *had* noticed. However difficult it might have been to explain without telling what

94

had happened the day before, at least it would have meant getting a ride to school in a warm car.

By the time the school came into sight, she knew it would take more than a few Ice Devils or ex-friends to keep her from its central heating.

But this morning she saw no Devils. Their parking spaces were empty of Firebirds—or any other cars. Apparently no other drivers were willing to risk the Devils' wrath, should they show up after all. Maribeth hurried across the road and up the sidewalk, glancing back involuntarily at the school door as she heard tires squeal. But the car rounding the King Street corner was only a rusted-out Chevette, and she turned away with a strange mixture of relief and foreboding.

She was beginning to think she would prefer to have Christine where she could keep an eye on her.

Ellen and Crystal, already at their lockers when she reached hers, exchanged glances as she took off her lightweight coat and reached for her books, which someone had obviously rescued from the floor after she fled the day before. Ellen took a cautious step toward her. "So—how are you?"

"I'm fine. How are you?"

"You're not feeling—strange?"

"No stranger than usual."

"Oh, come on, Maribeth, you know what she means!" Crystal broke in from the other side. "The way you ran out yesterday—you have to admit, it was pretty weird."

"Look," Maribeth said, banging her locker shut for emphasis, "you're right, I acted spooky. But it was my first day back at school, and what with Christine and everything—I freaked out, OK? But it's over. I'm myself again. You don't have to walk around me on eggshells all day."

95

"Well, it's not really us we're worried about." Ellen's eyes strayed over Maribeth's shoulder.

"Then who—"

Crystal slid past, smiling brightly. "Got to run! Oh, hello, Adam."

"Ada—" Maribeth turned around and came face to chest, and then, when she looked up, face to face, with the boy who had rescued her from Rick, while Crystal sailed down the hallway behind him, giving Maribeth a big wink and a thumbs-up sign before turning the corner.

"Yeah, I gotta go, too," said Ellen. "See you in social. 'Bye!" Abruptly Maribeth and Adam were alone.

She realized her mouth hung open, so she closed it and swallowed. "Uh—hi."

"Hi." A pause. His brown eyes met hers briefly, then looked down. "I just wanted to—you know, see if you were all right."

"Fine," she said automatically, then mentally kicked herself and managed a smile. "I mean it. I really am fine. You must have thought I was mental yesterday."

"Well..." He smiled back, his face lighting up. "Now that you mention it..."

Maribeth laughed ruefully. "I'm sorry. It was just—a lot of things all at once. It had nothing to do with you."

"I'm glad."

The first bell rang, warning students they only had three minutes to get to class. Lockers slammed up and down the hallway. Maribeth and Adam didn't move.

"I really should go," she said. "I'm glad you—I mean, I wanted to apologize."

"Apology accepted." Adam grinned. "Forget it ever happened. As far as I'm concerned, we've just met."

"Good idea." Maribeth extended her hand. "Hi, I'm Maribeth Gayle."

"Adam Metcalfe." They shook.

"So, Adam, what grade are you in?"

"I'm a senior."

"New in Weyburn?"

"We moved here from Vancouver before Christmas. What grade are you in?"

"Eleven."

"New in Weyburn?"

"Actually, I've lived here all my life."

"No kidding?" A pause, then Adam's smile broadened. "Tell me, Maribeth Gayle, do you like science fiction movies?"

Maribeth's heartbeat quickened. "Love them."

"How'd you like to see one with me tonight?"

"Sure!"

"Great!" Adam tore a page out of one of his notebooks. "Write down your address, and I'll come get you about six-thirty."

Maribeth scribbled their house number and street. "Great."

"Great!"

She handed the paper back to him. "You already said that."

"Repetition is a time-honored literary technique for emphasizing an idea." Maribeth blinked, and Adam laughed and held up his textbook. "English 30."

A classroom door closed somewhere and Maribeth started and looked around. Except for them, the corridor was deserted. "I think—" she began—and was drowned out by the final bell.

"We should get to class!" Adam cried, and they dashed off in different directions.

But Maribeth found, when she did get to class, that she didn't even mind the slightly sarcastic welcome of her teacher—and for the first time since she woke in the hospital, Christine was the furthest thing from her mind.

13

Pyrophobia

Christine had apparently slipped Ellen and Crystal's minds, too, because at lunch all they wanted to talk about was Adam. "I can't believe your luck!" cried Ellen, pouring ketchup on her french fries. "Girls all over school would kill to get a date with him, but he takes one look at you and—boom!"

"It's a knack," Maribeth said modestly. "You either have it or you don't."

"It's the knight-in-shining-armor syndrome, that's what it is." Crystal waved a forkload of chicken-fried steak to emphasize her point. "He saved you, he figures you owe him."

Maribeth laughed. "I'm going out with him because I like him, not because he rescued me from Christine's Jerks."

Ellen grinned. "Christine's Jerks! I like that."

"Just don't let Christine hear you say it," Crystal warned.

"She was after Adam for a while, too, you know," Ellen told Maribeth. "Just after he got here. While you were—uh—"

"Away?"

"Yeah. But she was kind of weird about it, you know? Like she was looking for someone to take the place of poor Tom."

"So Adam dodged her?"

"Never even knew he was in her sights, as far as I could tell." Ellen gulped down a french fry and reached for her

99

apple juice. "You know how blind guys are. But all the girls knew about it."

Oh boy, Maribeth thought. *Just what I need—something else to make Christine mad at me.* And worse, now she couldn't think about Adam without also thinking about Christine, whom she didn't particularly want to think about. However...

"Where is Christine today, anyway?" she asked, taking a casual swig of milk.

Crystal dabbed her glossy-pink lips with her napkin and said, "Who knows? She's out of school more than she's in, these days. I figure she'll be ·expelled before the end of January."

"But where does she go?"

"Regina, I hear," said Ellen. "She and the Devils—I mean, the Jerks—tear off up there every so often. Getting lessons in being a gang, I guess. They've had more experience up there in the semi-big city."

It sounded peculiar to Maribeth, but she wasn't going to look a gift horse in the mouth. If Christine was out of town, she didn't have to worry about her for the rest of the day—or, more importantly, that night.

School over, she hurried home, properly dressed in her winter coat and gloves this time, and rushed upstairs to shower and shampoo and begin the all-important process of deciding what to wear.

Wrapped in her bathrobe, her hair in a towel, she was on her way back to her room when she stopped at the head of the stairs and sniffed.

Smoke!

Her heart leaped in her chest and she raced downstairs, the burning smell strengthening until she burst into the kitchen. Flames shot from a metal trash can in the center of the room, while Sean, at the sink, frantically filled a pitcher. At the sight of the fire Maribeth froze, a wave of terror rushing through her. She clung to the doorjamb, staring at the flames; and for a moment, as Sean turned with the pitcher and dumped it into the trash can, she thought he was in the fire, and the flames were no longer yellow, but red—or green...

The fire vanished in billowing steam. Sean staggered back and set the pitcher on the cabinet, then leaned against it, his breath whooshing out. "I never thought it would flare up like that...."

With the fire out, Maribeth's fear subsided. Anger rushed in to take its place. "What were you doing?" she cried. "Trying to burn the house down?"

"No! I was just—I had to burn something, that's all, and I thought if I put it in the trash can from Dad's study, it would be all right—I've seen them do it on TV!"

"What do you mean, you had to burn something?" Maribeth crossed to the trash can, bent down, and pulled out the charred and soggy remains of a magazine. She could just make out long blonde hair and one half-closed woman's eye, underneath five remaining letters: AYBOY. "Sean!"

"A kid at school had half a dozen of them!" Sean cried. "He put one in my locker! I didn't want some teacher or somebody to see it there, and I couldn't leave it lying around the house, so I decided I had to burn it. That's all!"

"And I suppose you didn't even look at it, first?" Maribeth said drily.

"Well..."

She laughed, and dumped the magazine into the almost-full plastic bag in the utility room, then poured out the ash-stained water.

Sean watched her warily. "You won't tell Mom and Dad, will you?"

101

"I should—but you're lucky. I'm in a good mood. As long as you take out that trash bag with your little friend's 'gift' in it, then wash this can and put it back where you found it, I'll give you a break. But if they spot something, and ask me questions—"

"They won't!" Sean hurried to tie off the trash bag and get rid of the incriminating evidence before their parents came home.

Maribeth made her way back upstairs, her amusement at her brother's escapade slowly giving way to worry over her own reaction to the fire. She'd never been afraid of fire before—not like that—not like it was a dangerous snake under her bed, or a poisonous spider in her hair—as though it could somehow escape from the trash can and leap at her. She'd been so afraid she hadn't been able to move, to do anything. If something else had caught on fire, she was afraid she would have stayed right where she was and watched the house burn around her.

It must be because of the accident, she thought as she entered her room. She closed the door behind her, then took the towel off her head and sat down in front of the mirror to brush out her long hair. For just a moment she paused, looking at her image as though it belonged to someone else; then she blinked and everything was as it should be.

If I am going to go crazy, she told herself firmly, reaching for her brush, *it better not be until after tonight.*

She finally descended, wearing her best designer jeans and her favorite pale green blouse. Her father, sitting on the living room couch reading the newspaper, looked up and gave a low whistle. "I don't suppose you're dressed like that just to sit here and watch television with us this evening."

"No, Daddy. I have a date." She went into the living room and sat on the arm of the couch.

"So much for finding it hard to get back in the swing of things, eh?"

Maribeth thought about Christine and the Ice Devils, but all she said was, "I guess I was worried about nothing."

"Supper's ready!" called her mother, and her father put aside the paper and stood up, then pulled Maribeth to her feet and propelled her, laughing, into the kitchen.

"Guess what, Deb! Our little girl has a date."

"Oh?" Her mother set a steaming casserole dish on the table. "Anyone we know?"

"I don't think so." Maribeth slid onto her seat. "He's pretty new. He wasn't there before...back when school started."

"What's his name?" asked her father. "Sean! Supper, boy!"

"Adam. Adam Metcalfe. He's a senior."

"Oh, really? Going out with older men, eh?"

"Dad!"

Sean scurried in and took his place, looking, Maribeth thought, no more guilty than he usually did. Her mother sat down, and they all bowed their heads while her father said a brief prayer of thanks. When it was finished Maribeth caught Sean's eye across the table and winked. He looked away quickly.

"You should thank Sean," Maribeth's mother told her husband. "For once he carried out the trash without being asked."

Her father glanced at Sean, eyes wide. "A miracle!"

"Aw, Dad, cut it out," Sean mumbled. Maribeth kicked him under the table and he glared at her.

"So tell us more about this Adam," said Maribeth's mother, passing her the casserole. "He's new, you say. Where's he from?"

"Vancouver."

"Why did his family move to Weyburn?"

"I only talked to him for a few minutes, Mom. I didn't have time to get his whole life story."

"He asked you out after only a few minutes?"

"Boy has good taste," put in her father. "Pass the potatoes."

"Where are you going?" her mother went on.

Maribeth sighed. "To a movie."

"What's playing?"

"I don't know. Some science fiction flick. Why?"

"Just curious." Her mother put a dollop of beans on her plate.

"Your mother," said her father in a conspiritorial whisper, "is just being a mother."

"He's a perfectly nice guy, Mom—you'll see," Maribeth said. Sean opened his mouth, but Maribeth glanced toward the sink and he closed it again.

"I'm sure he is," her mother said. "It's just that—well, it's the first time you've been out since...you know."

"No party, no drinking, no fast driving." Maribeth held up three fingers in a Girl Guide salute. "Just me and a boy. What kind of trouble could we possibly get into?" Her parents gave her identical incredulous looks, and she laughed.

Adam arrived right on time. "You look great!" he told Maribeth as she opened the door.

"Thanks. So do you." And he did, Maribeth thought, even though he only wore ordinary blue jeans and a heavy blue coat. He would look great no matter what he wore. Definitely easy on the eyes.

Her mother emerged from the living room and her father from the kitchen, where he was washing dishes. "So, you must be Adam!" he said, coming forward with one soapy hand outstretched.

"Yes, sir." Adam shook hands firmly, ignoring the suds.

"John Gayle. This is my wife, Deb."

"How do you do?" Adam shook her hand, too.

"We should get going, shouldn't we?" Maribeth said anxiously, getting her own coat out of the hall closet, afraid her mother would start grilling Adam at any moment.

"Yes," said Adam. "Allow me." He held her coat while she slipped it on, then turned back to her parents. "It was nice meeting you, Mr. and Mrs. Gayle."

"You, too, Adam," said Mr. Gayle. "Have a good time."

"Not too good," Maribeth heard her mother murmur under her breath, and quickly herded Adam out the door.

"I like your parents," Adam said as he led Maribeth down the walk to his car, a gray Mustang.

"Well, you handled them just right," said Maribeth. "Mom was afraid I might be going out with a drunk, an addict or a sex maniac—or maybe all three. She's got this tendency to be kind of overprotective, especially since—the accident."

"I can understand that." Adam opened the passenger-side door and held it while she got in, then closed it, rounded the car and climbed in beside her. "I've only known you two days, and I feel protective toward you, too."

"For which I was very grateful yesterday," Maribeth said.

"What time am I supposed to have you back?" Adam turned the key and the engine rumbled to life.

"I turn into a pumpkin at midnight."

"Well, don't worry. You can trust Prince Charming to meet the deadline!" He shifted and pressed the accelerator, and the Mustang sped away from the curb.

14

The Note

At a quarter to twelve, Adam's Mustang rolled back up to the curb in front of Maribeth's house. "Here you are," he said. "Back from the ball with glass slippers intact."

Maribeth laughed. She had laughed a lot that night, at the movie, afterward at McDonald's, and then in the car, as they had sat and talked up on South Hill, looking out over the city lights from the park next to the hospital. "I really had a wonderful time. Thank you."

"Wonderful enough to want to do it again?"

She pretended to consider. "Well, my social calendar is really full..."

"Next weekend?"

"I think I can squeeze you in."

"I'll walk you to the door."

It was a short walk; on the porch, they paused. Maribeth turned to Adam. "Well," she said, and for some reason her voice was husky. "Good night, I guess."

"Good night," he said.

He was very close; and then a moment later he was even closer, as he kissed her.

She felt herself responding to him, her mouth opening to his, her arms going around him; but suddenly, from out of nowhere, fear and shame rose in her, and she broke off the kiss in confusion and pulled away. Adam blinked at her. "What—"

"I—I'm sorry," she stammered. "I can't—I—"

"Maribeth—" He moved closer.

"No!" she cried, then spun, fumbled the door open and rushed through, slamming it behind her, catching a last glimpse of Adam's bewildered face in the yellow glow of the porch light.

She leaned back against the door, shaking. Miser clattered out of the kitchen and padded down the hallway to greet her, and she knelt and hugged him, fondling his long, silky ears, until, after what seemed a long time, she heard the Mustang roar away, tires squealing, telling the whole neighborhood just how Adam felt.

She barely noticed, a few seconds later, the deep-throated rumble of another powerful car driving slowly past.

Everyone else was already in bed. No one saw her as she turned out the hall light and slowly mounted the stairs to her room, her make-up and her evening in ruins.

And the worst of it was, she didn't know why. There was no reason for her outburst that she could understand, nothing in her memory. She'd dated before, she'd kissed before, and except for that one time with Rick, it had never frightened her. She hadn't intended to kiss Adam, it had just happened, but it had been wonderful—for about five seconds. Then the strangeness had taken over, as it had time and time again since she woke, and spoiled everything.

He'll never want to see me again, she thought miserably. *And I really liked him. I really liked him. Maybe even...*

But she couldn't bring herself to think that she was falling in love with him, for that would have made the whole disaster too much to bear.

It was almost too much anyway. She washed the make-up from her face, undressed and climbed into bed, where she lay staring up at the ceiling and the bluish streak cast through a gap in her curtain by the streetlight outside. She wouldn't tell her parents, she resolved, just as she hadn't told them about the other strange incidents. They would only worry, and maybe it wasn't anything to worry about. Before she'd involve them, she'd find out for herself.

It wouldn't be that hard to arrange. Monday afternoon she had two spare periods in a row. She'd go see Dr. Ryback. She couldn't deny it any longer; she needed help.

She rolled onto her side and, a long time later, finally slept.

The weekend dragged past. She called Dr. Ryback and set up an appointment for Monday. She half-hoped, half-feared Adam would call her; he didn't. She thought about calling him, but couldn't bring herself to. If something were wrong with her, what had happened would only happen again, and Adam didn't deserve that. She'd wait.

She only hoped, if she were able to put a stop to whatever was going on, that he would still be interested.

Her parents queried her about her date, of course; she told them everything had been wonderful—which it had, until the last minute. But she remained vague on the question of whether she and Adam would be seeing each other again, and finally even her mother gave up. Sean teased her once or twice, but all she had to do was mouth the word "Playboy" in his direction, and he fell silent in the interest of self-preservation.

Monday dawned bright and very cold; Maribeth set out for school with the kind of sick feeling in her stomach she usually got on days there were tests for which she was not prepared. She certainly wasn't prepared, but this time it wasn't tests in geometry, history or chemistry that faced her, but Christine, Adam and Dr. Ryback. She dreaded seeing any of them, for different reasons; but she didn't see how she could avoid it.

However, Christine was once again absent, and Adam, though she glimpsed him once at the far end of the hall, never crossed her path, whether deliberately or through luck she didn't know and didn't want to know. Whichever, it suited her purposes and mood.

Ellen and Crystal tried to pump her for details of her date with Adam, but she brushed them off almost rudely. Ellen looked dismayed. "Oh, come on, Maribeth, there must be something you can tell us. It can't have been that bad. What did you do?"

"Look, I don't want to talk about it, OK?" Maribeth slammed her locker door and stalked away, not even caring what stories her friends would concoct in the absence of facts. She had bigger things to worry about than high school gossip.

Classes crept by; finally it was time for her doctor's appointment. She walked downtown to the office Dr. Ryback shared with three other physicians, on the bottom floor of a four-story, nondescript brick building. She expected to have to wait for at least a few minutes, but the nurse ushered her into the doctor's office the moment she arrived, and she barely had time to begin her usual pastime of trying to decipher the diplomas on the walls before Dr. Ryback joined her.

"So how's it feel to be back among the living?" the doctor greeted her, smiling.

"Great—most of the time."

Dr. Ryback's smile slipped. "Most of the time?"

"That's what I'm here about." Maribeth blurted out all the strange things that had happened to her since she awoke, the dreams, the visions, the emotions and reactions that seemed to come on her from nowhere, as if they weren't even her own. The doctor listened in silence. "I'm scared, Dr. Ryback," Maribeth finished finally. "What if—what if something is wrong with me, inside my head? What if

I—damaged something, somehow? Sometimes I think I'm going crazy!"

She stopped. Dr. Ryback doodled on a prescription pad on her desk for a moment. "Maribeth," she said finally, "I don't think you need me."

"But—"

"I'm not saying you shouldn't get help. Just not the kind I can give. I'm a medical doctor, a general practitioner and small-time surgeon; I fix broken bones and take out appendixes and watch over people who take two-month naps. I don't do voices and visions."

"But I hit my head—"

"That I can reassure you about. Maribeth, we carried out every test we could think of while you were unconscious. You weren't even here all the time; we took you to Saskatoon for more tests at University Hospital. They all told us the same thing; no significant neurological damage. You are not brain-damaged, Maribeth."

"Then why...?"

"Why is a big question. One you should certainly get answered." She paused. "I think you should see a psychologist."

"You mean I am going crazy?"

"No!" Dr. Ryback leaned forward quickly and put her hand on Maribeth's. "Of course not. But obviously something is troubling you. Something connected with the accident, I would guess—or something that happened just before it, in that time you can't remember. Psychologists have ways to penetrate that curtain you've pulled over those few hours, Maribeth. If you can find out what has disturbed you so much, then you can face it, and learn to live with it consciously—and your subconscious won't try to do it for you with false alarms and hallucinations."

For a moment Maribeth stared blankly at a print of an ancient Chinese acupuncture chart over the doctor's head, feeling hollow. "All right," she said finally. "Can you recommend someone?"

"As it happens..." Dr. Ryback ripped off the doodled-on page of the prescription pad and scrawled a name on the clean sheet underneath. She tore that one off, too, and handed it to Maribeth. "He works out of the Mental Health Centre. Tell him I recommended him." She looked hard into Maribeth's eyes. "And Maribeth, I really think you should tell your parents. You'll need their support if you're going to get over this problem."

"But I don't want them to worry! They worried about me for two months while I was in hospital. After I was home, everything was supposed to go back to normal—"

"Worrying is what parents are for, Maribeth. This problem isn't going to go away by itself. It will only get worse unless you do something about it. You're young; you need to put what happened behind you. But as long as you're having episodes like you've described to me, that accident is ruining your life. Tell your parents—and go see Dr. Westborg. Soon."

Maribeth looked at the slip of paper: it bore a phone number, and the name Dr. Julius Westborg, Weyburn Mental Health Centre, in Dr. Ryback's surprisingly legible handwriting. "All right."

"Good girl." Dr. Ryback stood, and so did Maribeth. "And good luck," the doctor added, shaking Maribeth's hand. "If you need me..."

"Thank you." Maribeth pocketed the note and went out.

She walked home hunched over to keep the bitter wind out of her face, her gloved hands thrust deep into the pockets of her coat. Somehow she had hoped that Dr. Ryback would be able to fix everything in one afternoon. Instead, she would have to see yet another doctor, for who knew how long, and involve her parents—and Adam would never want to go out with her again if he knew she was seeing a psychologist. If the kids at school found out...

She intended to talk to her parents that night, but somehow the time never seemed right, and Tuesday, Wednesday and Thursday also slipped by without her taking Dr. Westborg's number out of her desk drawer. During those three days nothing strange happened in her head, or at school, and she began to hope she had seen the last of it.

But early Friday morning she woke sweating, tangled in her bedclothes, a scream clawing at her throat, a vision of something black and malevolent, surrounded by blood-red flames, etched in her mind as though flash-photographed. A powerful car engine throbbed in the street outside, then suddenly roared and dwindled rapidly.

Maribeth lay back down and swallowed hard. She'd put it off as long as she could; it was time to call Dr. Westborg.

With that bleak thought still firmly in her mind, she went off to school, one week after her disastrous date with Adam, in a grim mood that even a balmy wind and the pink flush of sunrise couldn't lift. As always, she looked ahead at the Ice Devils' parking spaces, but the Firebirds were still missing; no one had seen the Devils or Christine since the first day of the semester.

Inside, Maribeth scanned the crowded hallways for Adam, but though she thought she glimpsed him entering the library, when she went past the door and looked in through the big windows, she couldn't see him.

If I wasn't crazy, we'd be going out again tonight, she thought miserably. Maybe...but she remembered her dream, and resolved anew, fiercely, to call Dr. Westborg when she got home that afternoon. Dr. Ryback was right; she couldn't let that accident ruin the rest of her life, or she'd end up like—like Christine.

She reached her locker, dialed the combination, and swung open the door. A folded piece of yellow paper slid out and fell to the floor, and she bent over to pick it up, puzzled; she didn't own any yellow paper.

The moment she read what was written on it her heart started to beat faster and her hand trembled slightly.

"I'm sorry about last Friday," it read. "We have to talk. Meet me at 982 16th St. at 11. Adam."

He was sorry! Maribeth looked at the address. That must be where he lives, she thought, then frowned; it was so far out on the northern edge of town she'd have to either borrow one of her parents' cars—which would mean answering too many questions—or take a taxi from somewhere she could walk to. And why so late?

She shook her head. It didn't matter. She would have met Adam in an alley if he'd asked. After a week, she no longer felt like avoiding him; she missed him too much. Instead, she wanted the chance to explain. If he knew she was doing something about her problem, maybe he wouldn't dump her. Just maybe...

She folded the precious piece of paper and thrust it into her purse, then snatched the books she needed from the locker, closed it and locked it and hurried to class.

15

Trapped

When she got home from school, Maribeth went straight to the phone—and hesitated. Maybe she didn't need to call Dr. Westborg. Maybe now that Adam—

No, that's stupid, she scolded herself. *How do you know what happened last time won't happen again?*

But what really made her pick up the phone was the realization that she couldn't apologize to Adam and tell him she was getting help unless she really *was* getting help.

In five minutes she had an appointment with Dr. Westborg for two o'clock the next day. Dr. Ryback, Dr. Westborg told her, had already contacted him, and he was breaking a long-standing rule about Saturday appointments just to see her. He didn't sound particularly upset about it, though, and as she hung up she found herself almost looking forward to meeting the man who owned the cheerful voice on the phone.

She just hoped no one but Adam ever found out about it.

Maribeth moved through the normal evening routine by rote, her mind much more on Adam than on her actions, a fact her father called to her attention gently as she was about to fill the salt shaker with sugar. "Earth to Maribeth," he said, covering the mouth of the shaker with his hand.

Maribeth realized what she was doing and laughed. "Sorry." She corrected the mistake and took the salt shaker to the table. She and her father were the only ones in the house; her mother had had to work late, and Sean was sleeping over at a friend's. By way of celebration, her father had made his special barbecued-without-a-barbecue hamburgers and home fries, and he set the two platters triumphantly on the table as Maribeth opened the refrigerator.

"So, what are your plans tonight?" her father asked as she reached for the ketchup, and she jumped.

"Why?" Her voice sounded unnatural to herself.

Her father looked surprised. "Just curious. I thought you might have another date with—Adam, was it?"

"Oh—well, as a matter of fact, I do." Flustered, Maribeth set the ketchup on the table and sat down in a hurry. "Ready to eat?"

"In a minute." Her father opened the refrigerator and took out a Coke apiece. "There! The perfect American meal. Too bad we're Canadians." He bowed his head and said a quick prayer, then straightened and reached for the top hamburger. "So, where are you and Adam going?"

"Oh—nowhere in particular."

Her father laughed. "That was always one of my favorite places to go on a date, too. Well, never mind. Just remember, back by midnight."

Maribeth said nothing, but bit into her burger.

She thought at first she would have to somehow disappear for a few hours to preserve the illusion of having gone on a date, but her father took advantage of his unexpected solitude to go to one of the horror movies he enjoyed but his wife would have nothing to do with. Maribeth had only to call a taxi—then lighten her already far-from-hefty piggy bank to pay for it.

She dressed warmly in the layered clothing she sometimes went cross-country skiing in, thinking that Adam might rather talk to her outside, walking, than in his own

115

living room, then sat watching TV, alternately biting her nails and mentally scolding herself for doing so.

Finally it was 10:30, and she called the cab. Ten minutes later she climbed into the back seat and told the driver, "982 Sixteenth Street."

He looked a little puzzled. "I don't think there is a 982 Sixteenth Street. Are you sure about the address?"

"I'm sure," said Maribeth, who had read and reread Adam's note all evening in between watching car chases.

The cabbie shrugged. "OK, I'll give it a try."

They drove down First Avenue, past the fairgrounds, the new swimming pool, the Wheatland Souris Seniors Centre and Jubilee Park, then turned left on Sixteenth Street. They passed a couple of churches, rows of houses behind fences—Sixteenth had once marked the edge of town, and was more an access road than a residential street...and then the pavement gave way to gravel, and they were in the country. "See?" the driver called back. "If that house number you gave me was right, it should still be up ahead of us. But we're out of town..."

"Isn't there still a house up ahead?"

Maribeth hadn't been out this way very often, but she seemed to recall...

"Well, yeah, but I don't think it's the place you're looking for..."

He slowed. "That's it over there to the right." But it's deserted. Has been for a long as I can remember."

"Maybe my friend's parents are fixing it up. Drive closer."

"It's your nickle." The cab driver turned left and they nosed down an incline onto a narrow road. "Well, somebody's been along here—there's lots of tracks—but the house still looks deserted to me."

It sure does, Maribeth thought uneasily, leaning forward. It was a two-story wooden frame building set well back from the road. The driveway curved through head-high lilac bushes, wild and unkempt. Even over the rumble of the engine she could hear the rattle of their dry branches in the wind.

The cab stopped in front of the house, headlights starkly illuminating the peeling white paint of the sagging porch, the boarded-up windows, the twisted, rusted drainpipe swinging in the wind that chased swirls of snow over the drifted-in yard. The big front door stood open, revealing only blackness. Someone had crudely splashed red paint on one of the porch pillars to form the numerals "982."

She stared at that, feeling the first twisting of fear in her stomach.

"Look, kid, you want me to take you home?" the cabdriver asked. "I won't even charge you. It's no good staying here. Someone must be playing a joke..."

But then Maribeth glimpsed something else, half-hidden behind a dilapidated granary. She pointed at it. "Aim your lights over there."

The cabdriver grunted, but backed up the cab a few feet, swung it to the left—and lit up a gray Mustang.

"He is here!" Maribeth cried—then the uneasiness returned. Why was he here? This couldn't be his house. And why was his car parked way over there? What if it was a trap? What if Christine had found a way to get even with both of them?

"Look, kid, this is no place for you and your friends to be playing around," the cabbie said. "It's not safe—"

Maribeth made up her mind. "You're right. Could you stay—just for a few minutes—while I look around and see if I can find my friend? If I don't then I'll want a ride back into town."

"Sure, kid."

"Thank you." Maribeth opened the door and got out into the cold wind.

Behind her the cab chugged away, the steam of its exhaust whipped away almost before it could form. The cab's headlights still lit Adam's Mustang, but that spot of light only made the rest of the farmyard seem darker. Even the snow didn't help much, only confusing things, giving threatening shape and substance to the deep shadows. Maribeth wrinkled her nose at the smell of gasoline, and walked away from the cab.

But the smell didn't go away. In fact, it strengthened as she mounted the porch, half-expecting her foot to crash through the rotting wood. The black hole of the front entrance was doubly intimidating from closer up, and now the smell of gasoline was stomach-turning. "Adam?" Maribeth called, very softly, then cleared her throat and said more loudly, "Adam?"

She listened. Nothing. She took another couple of steps forward and leaned on the doorframe, poking her head into the chill blackness beyond. "Adam, I know you're here, I saw your car. Where are you?"

Was that a sound? She cocked her head. *Yes!* Like a moan—and suddenly she realized that it wasn't pitch-black inside the house after all, that a faint glow spilled down the stairs to her right. "Adam?"

It *was* a moan! Remembering the cabby's words about the old house not being safe, she had a sudden horrifying image of Adam somehow trapped beneath a fallen beam or stuck up to his chest in a hole in the floor. She hurried inside and up the stairs. This was no time to develop a fear of the dark, anyway—it had never bothered her before.

The smell of gasoline waned as she ascended, but the light strengthened, leaking out under a door at the head of the stairs that creaked open when she twisted its knob and pushed.

The room beyond was empty except for a flashlight hung on a rope, swinging in the wind, which moaned between the boards covering the glassless window opposite the door. Maribeth grabbed the flashlight and jerked it free of the rope. "That's not funny," she muttered, then froze as she heard muffled voices—followed by the unmistakable sound of the cab driving away.

Lighting her way with the flashlight, Maribeth dashed out of the room, her heart suddenly pounding; but as she reached the top of the stairs the front door banged shut, and something thudded against it. "Adam?" she called, but she didn't believe for a minute it was him. She clattered down the stairs.

Again she smelled gasoline, and yellow light glowed through the flyspecked panes of glass in the door. For a moment it illuminated a vague shape, too indistinct to identify—and then someone shouted, the dark shape leaned forward—

—and Maribeth screamed and stumbled back as flames exploded around the base of the door.

She turned and ran into the kitchen, but flames licked around the back door, too, and fiery light flickered between the boards over every window. Someone had doused the whole base of the house with gasoline and set fire to it, she realized in a daze, falling back against the counter and watching the first tendrils of flame running across the tiled floor.

Smoke choked her, and, coughing and gasping, she turned and ran again, through a short hallway under the stairs into yet another room. Here there were no doors and the air was clearer, but here, too, flames leaped beyond the windows, and smoke already curled across the ceiling.

And then she heard another moan, a real one, and ran through another doorway to her left, discovering a bathroom—and Adam, bound and gagged and lying in the bathtub. Blood from a cut over his left eye had soaked one side of the gag, but his eyes, widening at the sight of Maribeth, gleamed in the fiery light.

She felt—strange, disconnected. If she didn't free Adam, he would die, and so would she, but somehow she couldn't move. She clung to the doorjamb as the first flames burst from the wall over Adam's head and spread hungrily over the underside of the ceiling. Flowered wallpaper charred and flaked and dropped as hot ash on Adam, who struggled desperately, staring wide-eyed at Maribeth.

But her gaze was riveted on the fire, and somewhere deep inside her a horrible memory struggled to surface, something too terrible to be faced, something more terrible than the fire around her now. Something to do with Christine, with the accident, with Tom—

—Tom, who had burned to death in the wreckage of his car—

A big piece of paper, burning like a torch, peeled free of the ceiling and dropped toward Adam, who cringed back and struggled mightily, but could only flop like a fish.

The burning paper missed him, but where it landed the linoleum of the bathroom floor began to char.

Maribeth hardly noticed the intense heat and choking smoke. It was all receding from her, dwindling, as though seen through the wrong end of binoculars.

That's nice, she thought dreamily. *That's nice. I don't want to be here. I don't want to be here, and now I'm leaving it. Leaving it all behind...*

The horrible memory bubbled inside her. She caught a glimpse of it, just a glimpse, but that was enough.

Maribeth fled.

And Liothel suddenly jerked upright and took a deep, searing breath of smoke-filled air with lungs that were not her own.

16

Escape

Things that had seemed like a dream to Liothel suddenly became terrifyingly real. For a moment, like Maribeth before her, she clung helplessly to the doorjamb; then she met Adam's terrified gaze and forced her new limbs into action. She leaped forward, coughing, and freed Adam's hands, while the burning ceiling continued to drop hot ash on their heads. Adam jerked off the gag and started untying his feet. "It's about time!" he cried. "I thought for a minute you were going to let me roast!"

That wasn't me, it was Maribeth, Liothel thought. *I don't belong here. I shouldn't be here—*

"Jeez, Maribeth, don't just stand there! Move!" Free of his bonds, Adam scrambled out of the tub and pushed her into the larger room outside as the bathroom ceiling gave an alarming creak and started to sag. He stared around wildly. "There's got to be a way out—"

Liothel coughed and rubbed at her streaming eyes. *Trapped,* she thought almost hysterically. *Trapped like a soulworm in a Circle of Fire...Jara, you're supposed to be here, not me. What do I do? What's happening?*

"Maribeth!" Adam shook her, hard. "Maribeth, think. You've been through the house. There must be a way out. There must be! What about the back door?"

Liothel tried to reply, but the words wouldn't come. Instead she just shook her head, mutely.

"Come on, Maribeth, snap out of it! What else did you see?" Adam coughed. "Maribeth, please!"

Languages whirled in Liothel's mind, hers and Maribeth's, twisted, tangled...she forced herself to concentrate on what Maribeth had seen just before she had fled and Liothel had surfaced with such shocking abruptness. The downstairs was hopeless, every wall on fire, but upstairs...upstairs...

She tried to let go of her own language, to let Maribeth's brain and throat act freely, and choked out, "Upstairs. A window—"

"Come on!" Adam grabbed her hand and pulled her after him.

Flame sheathed one wall of the front room and billowed across the ceiling. The heat almost drove them back into the kitchen—but the flames were breaking through there, as well. Adam plunged ahead and Liothel followed blindly, through searing air, to the stairs and up them, Adam's footsteps clattering ahead of her, every breath burning her lungs.

Upstairs it was cooler but smokier. Liothel's head spun, and Adam pulled her down beside him as he dropped to his hands and knees. The air seemed a little clearer near the floor. "Where?" Adam yelled above the rising roar of the fire.

She tried to answer—couldn't—tried again. "Straight ahead!" She couldn't see the room where Maribeth had found the flashlight; everywhere she looked there was only the red-tinged fog of smoke. But it had been right at the top of the stairs —

Adam muttered to himself as he felt along the wall. Liothel took shallow breaths and fought rising panic. There had to be an opening, there had to be! She couldn't have gone that far wrong—

"In here!" Adam cried, and she felt for and grabbed his foot as he crawled forward.

The smoke was a little less dense beyond the door: she could vaguely see the outline of the room in the red glow from below. Adam lurched to his feet and ran to the window, pulling at the old boards that covered it. They resisted, until Liothel added her strength—or Maribeth's—to his. Then they gave, slowly at first, rusty nails screeching in protest, but finally breaking loose all at once and clattering to the floor.

Smoke rushed out through the gaping window, borne by a hot breeze at their backs. Liothel leaned out. Below them was the roof over the kitchen. Flame licked its edges, but it still looked solid. Adam pointed down. "Women and children first!"

Liothel hesitated, her mind seeking the reference in the unfamiliar paths of Maribeth's brain, then decided this was hardly the time to worry about it and clambered out feet first, lowering herself as far as she could before letting go.

She hit the roof hard and dropped to her knees, broken shingles skittering away to left and right. Quickly she crawled forward, taking deep gulps of clean air and coughing out smoke, and heard Adam swear as he crashed to the roof behind her. She glanced back to make sure he was all right, then crawled on to the end of the beam. No flames showed there yet, though the eaves to either side were already burning. She took a quick glimpse over the edge.

The wall beneath her was on fire. They had only a few minutes—maybe seconds—before the flames reached them.

"Go on!" Adam shouted to her as something inside the house collapsed with a roar, and smoke and flames suddenly shot out of the window from which they had jumped. Hot sparks showered them. "I'm right behind you!"

Liothel looked down again. A snowdrift curved around the base of the wall, but it didn't look very deep. And there could be no lowering herself gradually this time; she'd toast her feet.

"What are you waiting for?" Adam yelled.

Good question, Liothel thought; and stood up, took a deep breath, and jumped.

It was over in a second: a dizzying rush of air, hot then cold, the ground leaping up at her, and then she plunged into the snow and fell forward. Ice filled her mouth and nose and eyes, but she revelled in its crisp coolness after the lung-searing heat and smoke.

Adam hit the drift beside her with a muffled thump. She rolled over, blinking, and watched the fire race up the side of the kitchen. The first flames broke through the kitchen roof.

A distant siren pierced the fire's roar. Liothel sat up suddenly as Maribeth's memories identified the sound for her. Her mind was beginning to function more clearly in its new habitation, and she stumbled only a little over the words as she said, "Adam, we've got to get out of here!"

"What are you talking about?" he said, also sitting up in the snow. "We've got to tell the police and fire department what happened—"

"No!"

"But—"

"Please, Adam. I'll try to explain later—I promise. But for now—please, let's get out of here!"

He stared at her for a moment, the whites of his eyes startling in his otherwise soot-begrimed face, then shook his head, muttered, "I must be crazy," and scrambled to his feet. "Come on, then," he snapped, and ran toward his Mustang.

Liothel dashed after him. The car's powerful engine started at once, and a moment later they roared down the twisting access road in the dark, headlights off, Liothel's hands gripping the edge of the seat like vises. She had Maribeth's memories of riding in these magical wagons, but memories were hardly the same as—she gasped as the car skidded onto the main road, and raced away from the flashing red and blue lights coming up Sixteenth Street.

Behind them, the roof of the house caved in, pouring smoke and sparks into the sky, the wind sending tiny red stars dancing across the road. Flames roared up as though trying to touch the aurora borealis that now glowed in the northern heavens. The light of stars and aurora, reflected from the snow, made the road a featureless black stripe painted across the icy blue-green plain. "I swear, Maribeth, you'd better have a good explanation—" Adam growled.

How about the fact I'm not really Maribeth? Liothel thought. *Not that I can tell you that...*

They turned left onto another gravel road, and Adam turned on his lights and accelerated, driving until the burning house was only a red spark on the horizon behind them. "Where to now?" he asked finally, slowing.

Liothel thought desperately. Maribeth had told her parents she was—going out on a date? (There were memories underlying that concept Liothel was not prepared to deal with yet.) Her father had told her to be home by—

"What time is it?"

Adam pointed to a digital clock on the dashboard. "Just after midnight."

"Please take me home." *Mykia, if you can manage it,* she thought miserably.

"Home?"

"Mari—uh, my parents—will—" She searched for the correct phrase. "They'll ground me if I break curfew."

"And how are you going to explain looking like a toasted marshmallow?"

"I'll just have to hope they won't see me, that's all."
At least the language was coming more easily all the time,
Liothel thought. But her mind bubbled like a cauldron, full
of conflicting thoughts and memories and images. Only with
an effort of will was she able to control herself, to keep
from collapsing into a quivering, sobbing heap.

"Uh-huh." Adam slowed and pulled off onto a field
access, but didn't turn the car around. Instead he looked at
Liothel, his face illuminated by the blue glow of the
instrument lights. "You've got to tell me what's going on,"
he said quietly. "You've got to, or I've got to go to the
police. Somebody tried to kill us tonight."

Liothel forced herself to concentrate. "You know who
it had to be."

"I suspect the Ice Devils, and your 'friend' Christine.
But I never actually saw anyone. Did you?"

Had she? She thought about it, then shook her head.
"What were you doing there?" She asked the question that
had been foremost in Maribeth's mind.

"What were you doing there?" Adam countered.

"Ma—I got your note."

"And I got yours."

"But I never wrote one!"

"Neither did I." He sighed. "I got a note saying you
were sorry about—about what happened—and asking me to
meet you at 982 Sixteenth Street at 10:30. The street
numbers didn't go that high, but I saw that old house a little
further out in the country and decided that must be the place.
When I got there, though, it looked deserted. I parked the
car, got out, started toward the house—and someone hit me
over the head." He touched the back of his skull gingerly.
"When I woke up, I was in that bathtub and the house was
on fire."

Liothel told him how Maribeth had come to be there, while the larger portion of her mind marvelled at how sane and rational she sounded, when underneath she trembled with confusion. For the moment she could run on what Maribeth would have called autopilot. With the initial shock over, the memories she shared with Maribeth from the last few days and her increasing confidence with the language allowed her to act almost normal.

But she couldn't keep it up for long. She needed time to sit down and come to terms with everything that was in her—in Maribeth's—head. Her memories of Mykia were clear, but even clearer, at the moment, were all of Maribeth's memories. It was as if she had lived two separate lives which had only come together in the last few days. She didn't know how to deal with it, how to make use of it—or what to do when and if she finally did know those things.

And deep down was a hideous truth she hardly dared think about yet—the reason the Warders had tried to send Jara here—the soulworm. Liothel was convinced she knew whom it had possessed; everything Maribeth remembered about Christine from the last few days pointed to Christine being the creature's host. It lurked within her, building its strength, biding its time until it could find or trigger the violence it needed to spawn. Jara would have known how to deal with it; but Liothel was only an Acolyte, with no powers of Exorcism—or anything else. She didn't have the skills to save this world. But she was there, and Jara was not, and one thing she remembered clearly from all the discussion in Mykia—only one Warder at a time could come through the Gate.

Her duty was clear—but nothing else was. How could she fight the soulworm with none of the Warders' powers? Especially when the soulworm already knew she was there. It must have sensed her presence, even hidden beneath Maribeth's personality, the moment Christine first laid eyes on her. That had to be the reason behind the attempt on her and Adam's lives. It had tried to win the war before battle was even joined, while its adversary was incapacitated. It had failed—but it would try again. Liothel, and Maribeth, and Adam, too, it seemed, were all in danger—and there was nothing she could see to do about it. Bitterness rose in her throat. Her failure to Manifest would cost her more than the sting of the younger Acolytes' remarks this time.

Something must have shown on her face, because Adam suddenly leaned toward her. "Are you all right?"

"Please take me home," she said in a small voice. *All the way home,* she pleaded silently to the Creator.

But all that happened was that Adam put the car in gear and turned it toward town, taking a road that didn't take them past the scene of the fire.

He said nothing until he parked in front of Maribeth's house, then reached out and touched Liothel's arm as she started to get out of the car. She flinched.

"You're tense as a guitar string," he said. "Maribeth, please. Tell me the truth about what's going on. Otherwise I will go to the police. I'll have to!"

Liothel found her voice. "Please, wait," she whispered. "I promise, I will tell you—everything—but I have to sort it all out in my head. I can't—not right now—I can't tell you." *Because I don't know what to do!* she cried silently.

"They tried to kill us! We can't just ignore—"

"But we don't have any proof of who did it. You said yourself you didn't see anybody—and neither did I."

"It must have been the Devils." He released her arm. "But I admit I don't know why."

"I think I do." She held up her hand as he started to speak. "Just give me a little time, and I'll try to explain it to you. Please?"

"All right." Adam put his hands back on the steering wheel. "But if anything else happens—"

It will, Liothel thought. *It will. This is only the beginning.* She got out of the car. "Good night," she told Adam, and closed the door.

The Mustang's tires chirped as Adam drove away, and Liothel, feeling both as if she were coming home and as if she were hopelessly lost, walked slowly up the sidewalk.

17

Liothel's Dream

She—or Maribeth—was lucky; Maribeth's parents were either still out or asleep. She hoped they were out, because they were both light sleepers, and she had little hope of reaching Maribeth's room without one of them waking and looking at the clock to see what time it was.

But she wasn't *that* lucky; as she reached the head of the stairs Maribeth's mother called, "Maribeth? Is that you?"

No, she thought, but, "Yes," she said.

"It's almost one o'clock."

"I know—Mom. I'm sorry."

"We'll talk about it in the morning. Go to bed."

"Good night."

"Good night."

Liothel crept into Maribeth's room and started peeling off her smoke-, sweat- and soot-stained clothes, which she stuffed under the bed until she could decide what else to do with them. *Well*, she thought, *it could have been worse. Maribeth's mother could have come out and seen her daughter looking like last week's kitchen fire.*

Except, she thought with sudden dislocation, *they don't have kitchen fires here.* Instead they have—gas and electricity, and other things that Maribeth took for granted but that Liothel couldn't help thinking of as magic.

Of course, magic does have its good points, she thought a few minutes later as she luxuriated in an apparently inexhaustible shower of hot, clean water and washed the last of the grime from her skin and hair with sweet-scented soap that was a far cry from the harsh lye-based concoction she was used to.

But as she stepped out of the shower and reached for a towel, she glimpsed herself in the incredibly perfect mirror that faced the stall, and almost like a physical blow, realization hit her—she was living inside someone else's body.

Blonde hair instead of black, green eyes instead of blue, at least four inches more height and twenty-five more pounds, and curves to make a princess jealous. A beautiful body—but not hers.

She wrapped her robe around that strange new body and fled shivering to her room, where she burrowed under warm blankets in a wonderfully soft bed, but still couldn't stop shaking.

After she had hit her head and fallen through the Gate, there had been a long time from which all she remembered were confused, horrible dreams of flames and people burning. Then the dreams had changed, had become almost real, until finally she realized that she had made the transfer to another world that Jara had been supposed to make, that she was in the body of another girl.

But she hadn't been able to affect anything, and part of the time what she had seen had been strangely fuzzy, as though she were looking at it through a badly made spyglass. Even when everything was clear, she had felt distant from it, as distant as she had felt from her own body, wherever it might be, and from the mission that she had unwittingly usurped, to find the soulworm that had fled into this world.

That had all changed when Maribeth's consciousness had fled in terror from the fire—the fire set by the soulworm's possessed host, Maribeth's once-best friend, Christine Redpath.

Liothel frowned, doubting her own conclusions for a moment. How could she be so sure? Of course, Christine had been hateful to Maribeth, and the members of her gang had been worse, but still, the soulworm could be in someone else, someone unsuspected...

But her mind wouldn't accept the possibility. She thought back, trying to find in Maribeth's memories something the girl whose body she wore had overlooked, or pushed out of her mind. It was like looking through a library of familiar books that had been reorganized by a stranger. Everything was there, but...

An image appeared. She saw it as clearly as though it hung in the air before her: Christine, surrounded by blood-red flames, glowing with malevolent power. Liothel's eyes widened as she recalled what Jara had taught her:

"To some it looks like a fire shining through the skin, as though they're burning from the inside out. That's what it's like for me. Others see it differently—as lightning wreathing the body, or as nothing more than an evil glow—but for those with the Gift, it is always there, unless the soulworm tries to hide it; then it becomes a question of the relative strengths of soulworm and Warder. If the soulworm is not concerned about being detected, it's as clear as daybreak."

Liothel sat up slowly and stared wide-eyed into the darkness. *I've Manifested!* she realized in wonder. *Detection! Even in this body...*

But the elation she should have felt, would have felt had the Manifestation taken place back in Mykia as it should have long ago, barely began before dying in the bleak knowledge that nothing had changed. Even without the Talent, she could have deduced—had deduced—that the soulworm possessed Christine. She didn't need the Gift of Detection—she needed the Gift of Exorcism. Jara had been chosen because she was dual-talented. Liothel wasn't—and thus the very thing she had longed for in Mykia only emphasized her inadequacy here. She was as useless here as she was in Mykia. The only thing she could hope to accomplish would be to get herself and her unwitting host killed.

Christine had already made a good attempt, knowing that if she killed Maribeth, with Liothel inside, Liothel would...

Would what? No one in Mykia had discussed the possibility. Would she die with Maribeth or simply return to her own body?

If that's true, at least I know I can get back, she thought, then flushed. If she believed that, she might risk Maribeth's life foolishly. Maribeth hadn't asked to become involved; Liothel wished there were some way she could talk to the other girl, tell her what was happening. But where Maribeth had gone, Liothel could neither sense nor follow.

She was risking Maribeth's life enough just by being there. The soulworm in Christine, fascinated, like so many of its kind, with its own ultimate nemesis—fire—had tried to burn Maribeth alive, knowing that was what Liothel intended for it. Except, without an Exorcist...unwillingly Liothel recalled her conversation with Jara shortly before the ill-fated opening of the Gate. Without an Exorcist at hand, there was only one way to destroy the soulworm—to burn its host with it inside.

More than just "its host," Liothel thought harshly. *Christine—Maribeth's best friend.* Lying in Maribeth's bed, in Maribeth's body, she shuddered. Unwittingly, Maribeth and Christine had become pawns in a battle that had begun in another world. It might have made a wonderfully tragic tale for telling around the fire late at night; but in real life, the tragedy was too great to bear. "I can't do it," Liothel whispered fiercely. "I can't! She's Maribeth's friend. She's possessed. It's not her fault!"

But inexorably her conscience reminded her of her vows as an Acolyte. Jara, dear, kind Jara, had been prepared to do what must be done—if Liothel could not, then it would be the ultimate proof of what she had secretly felt for years—that she would never be a Warder, that she couldn't be. Manifesting her Gift would mean nothing if she failed in this task she had usurped through her own clumsiness. The soulworm would wreak havoc in this already violent world—a world, Liothel knew from Maribeth's memories, that now had weapons to destroy entire cities—if it were allowed to spawn. And spawn it would, soon, as soon as it had fed sufficiently on the negative emotions it was using its unwitting servants, the Ice Devils, to create. Once it had the strength, it would force some kind of physical violence, something to generate the anger and bloodlust it needed to engorge itself and multiply, and then there would be a dozen soulworms, and then a hundred, ten thousand, a million—and this world would be engulfed in bloodshed to make the worst already recorded in its history pale into insignificance.

And it would all be the Warders' fault for opening the Gate that should not have been opened...

No, Liothel thought grimly. *It would be my fault.*

She was fortunate, she supposed, that the contact point between the worlds was here, in this small, peaceful city. Had it been in—Bosnia, Maribeth's memories supplied—the soulworm might have already overrun the planet. Here, it would take longer. But not too long, Liothel knew. If she were going to act, it would have to be soon.

If my Gift had to manifest here, O Creator, she whispered in prayer, *why could You not have made me an Exorcist, as well as a Detector? Must Christine really die for me to save her world? Must my vows to You make me a killer?*

That terrible question, hanging in her mind, kept sleep at bay for a long time.

Liothel woke late in the morning and for a moment stared blankly at the bright walls and peculiar pictures. Where were the familiar stone blocks, the rush-strewn floor?

But the moment of disorientation passed quickly and she swung her feet out of bed. Today she would have to talk to Adam—and somehow stop him from going to the police. That would only complicate things. The soulworm would be anxious—doubly so, when it found out she and Adam had escaped its trap. If pressed too hard it might even abort its spawning here, flee to some other site where Liothel could never find it. It had to be stopped here, now, by her.

She couldn't involve Adam, either, she decided as she tied her shoes, or tried to; it wasn't until she quit watching her fingers and let them do the task on their own that she succeeded. She wished more than anything that she did not have to involve Maribeth, either. In fact, what she wished most of all was that she didn't have to involve herself.

Glumly she padded down the stairs to the kitchen, to be greeted by Maribeth's mother, who was baking cookies. "Well, young lady," she said as Liothel entered the room and followed Maribeth's instincts to the refrigerator, "what do you have to say for yourself?"

For a moment Liothel stared at her blankly; then remembered that Maribeth had broken curfew. "Oh! Mom, I'm sorry, I just..."

"Let me guess. Adam ran out of gas? There were submarine races in the river?"

Liothel blinked. "Submarine races" didn't mean anything even to Maribeth. "No, Adam had plenty of gas. We just...misjudged the time."

"Hmmm." Maribeth's mother cracked two eggs into the batter. "You know what this means, of course."

She did? Liothel thought carefully, then winced. *Yes, she did.* She'd told Adam the night before, speaking from Maribeth's memories, that she would be grounded if she was late; now she fully grasped the strange term's meaning, and blurted, "Mom, no! You can't ground me!"

"Can't I?" Maribeth's mother put the bowl of batter under the mixer. "We made an agreement at the beginning of the year as to what your hours were to be. You agreed midnight on weekends was reasonable unless you got prior permission to stay out later. You told your father last night you'd be home by twelve. You didn't come home until one. And you know what punishment we agreed on: grounded for one week for every hour you're late."

"But—Mom, I've got—"

"One week, Maribeth. Starting from today."

Frustration boiled up in Liothel, and she slammed the door of the refrigerator and stalked out of the kitchen. She stomped back up the stairs to her room, kicked the door closed behind her, then flounced down on the bed. One week stuck in the house after school and every night. Who knew what the soulworm might accomplish in one week? "Stupid woman," she muttered. "She's risking the whole world because her daughter broke a silly rule."

Someone knocked on the bedroom door. "Go away!" Liothel yelled.

"It's Mom. May I come in?"

Liothel opened her mouth to say no, then shut it again, her anger subsiding into shame. *This isn't my house*, she reminded herself. *They don't even know I'm here.* "Of course—Mom."

Mrs. Gayle opened the door and stepped in, wiping her floury hands on her apron. "Maribeth, what's wrong?"

"Nothing." Liothel wondered if lying was lying when you did it with someone else's tongue.

137

"Nothing? You made butter out of the cream in the door of the refrigerator and came close to scrambling our breakfast eggs for the next week. And I could still see your footprints in the carpet on the stairs."

"I'm sorry," Liothel mumbled, feeling like she had done something wrong and was letting someone else take the blame for it. "I was just—upset."

"Did something happen last night?"

Liothel tensed. "Something—happen?"

Maribeth's mother sat down beside her and put her arm around her. "With Adam. Did he try to make you do something you didn't want to do?"

Liothel opened her mouth; closed it again. Maribeth's memories weren't helping. What was her mother talking about?

"I don't understand."

"Did he want to go farther than you did?"

Something suddenly surfaced from Maribeth's mind, and Liothel's reaction drove her cheeks, whether really hers or not, bright red. "No!" she burst out, and instantly realized how it must sound.

"I don't want you to be afraid to talk to me about it. I was your age once, you know. And things weren't that different twenty-five years ago. I know it's hard to believe, but whatever happened, you wouldn't shock me."

"Really—uh, Mom, nothing happened. Not like—that. We just—had a fight." She managed a weak smile. "That's all. It'll be all right. And so will I."

"You're sure?"

Liothel nodded.

Maribeth's mother gave her a hug, then kissed her forehead. "You know how much I worry about you. You're my little girl...I love you."

"I'm fine, Mom." Liothel swallowed. "Really, I am."

"I'm glad." Maribeth's mother stood. "But my cookies won't be fine if I don't get back down to them." She paused in the doorway. "You can still have breakfast if you want it."

"No—thanks. I'll wait until lunch."

"Okay."

After Mrs. Gayle left, Liothel stayed on the bed, her anger gone, feeling worse than ever. "You're my little girl...I love you," Maribeth's mother had said. How many times had Liothel wished she'd had a mother to tell her that? Maribeth did—a mother, a father, a brother; a close-knit family, a good family, a strong family—the kind of family Liothel had longed for all her life. They'd already lost Maribeth once, had been overjoyed when she returned to them.

Now she's gone again, and they don't even know it, Liothel thought miserably. *And even if she comes back, what I have to do will tear this family apart like nothing else has been able to.*

Because unless I can find a way out of it, I'm going to have to turn their "little girl" into a killer.

18

Menace At McDonald's

"Adam called," Maribeth's father said that night at supper. Liothel had spent a miserable slow day doing nothing but laundry (which pleasantly surprised Maribeth's mother while allowing Liothel to wash her smoke-stained clothes) and worrying, all the while expecting Adam to get in touch with her—and wondering what she would say to him. Now she stiffened.

"Why didn't you tell me?"

"I told him you were being punished because he brought you home late last night, and suggested whatever he had to say could wait until Monday at school. Pass the potatoes, please."

Liothel didn't move until Sean nudged her, then she mechanically handed the bowl across the table. Maribeth's father seemed to be waiting for more argument, but Liothel's mind was racing. Now she had a legitimate excuse for not talking to Adam. If she could avoid him at school, or use some pretense about her parents forbidding her to talk to him, she might be able to put off giving him any explanation until after she had done what she had to.

And then he won't want to see Maribeth, will he? an inner voice pricked her. *Even if he could—she'll be locked away, of course...*

"Maribeth?"

Liothel blinked and looked at Maribeth's father. "Sorry...?"

"I said you had another phone call, too." He poured gravy on the mound of mashed potatoes he had dipped from the bowl. "From a Dr. Westborg."

"Westborg?" Maribeth's mother frowned. "He's a psychologist."

"I always knew she was crazy," Sean put in, but subsided at a sharp glance from his father and an even sharper poke from Liothel, in response to some Maribeth-molded reflex that caught her off-guard.

"What did he want?" she asked as innocently as possible.

"He wanted to know why you didn't keep your appointment with him," Maribeth's father said quietly. "Why didn't you tell us?"

Liothel poked at her food, mind racing through Maribeth's memories. "I—didn't want to worry you."

"Honey, you know you can always come to us," said Maribeth's mother. "What's wrong?"

"It's just—I've been having a lot of bad dreams since the accident, that's all. Dr. Ryback suggested I talk to this Westborg guy. So I made an appointment. It's no big deal."

Maribeth's father frowned. "What kind of bad dreams?"

"Just—dreams. You know, about...what happened. I'd really—rather not talk about it." Liothel had no trouble sounding uncomfortable. She knew now, looking back, that her hidden presence in Maribeth's mind had caused most of the peculiar incidents that had prompted the other girl to seek help.

Most, but not all. There was something there, something deeper, something to do with the paralyzing fear that had driven Maribeth away and brought Liothel forward, something prompted by fire—but Liothel wasn't about to go to a psychologist, wearing Maribeth's body. The vague connotations the word conjured from Maribeth's memories made her uncomfortable. Who knew what other powers

141

psychologists had that Maribeth knew nothing of? He might be this world's equivalent of a Sentinel—able to tell that Maribeth was really Liothel. He might even have some way of driving her out of Maribeth's body; and if that happened, the soulworm had won.

The thought that at least then she'd be home crossed her mind, and she hurriedly took a bite of broccoli.

"Hmmm." Maribeth's father looked troubled. "All right, if you'd rather talk to a psychologist than to us—"

"It's not—"

"—then I guess we'll have to respect it. Dr. Westborg said he's booked up until next weekend at the same time. I told him you'd call him back Monday."

Liothel nodded, and the rest of the meal passed in uncomfortable silence. Maribeth's family gave her variously worried, puzzled or (in Sean's case) mischievously pleased glances. Liothel left the table as soon as she could.

She set out for school Monday morning, walking into the teeth of a bitter wind, wondering if she dared skip classes for the day, and finally deciding it would be noticed and Maribeth's parents would find out. Not only would she get the innocent Maribeth in trouble again, it would make it even harder for her to do what must be done: to turn the tables on the soulworm, to get it (she tried not to think of the creature in terms of its host, Christine) in the same kind of fiery trap into which it had lured her and Adam—and make sure that it, unlike them, did not escape.

Not that she knew how she could do that—or even if she could bring herself to.

Her problems multiplied the moment she set foot in the school, for there, waiting for her, was Adam.

For a moment she considered turning and running, but he grabbed her arm and dragged her into a corner, hemming her up against the school trophy case with one arm. "All right, you've had time to think," he said. "Now talk."

The warning bell rang.

"We're going to be late for class," Liothel said desperately.

"Dammit, Maribeth—"

"Look, we'll talk later. I promise—"

Adam didn't move. "When?"

"I don't know, just later." Students hurrying by gave them speculative looks. "Come on, Adam, if I'm late again—"

"What's your last class before lunch?"

"Huh? Uh—" Liothel racked Maribeth's brain. "This is Day 4, so it's...algebra."

"That's in D104, right?"

"Uh, yeah..."

"OK. I'll meet you there, and we'll go somewhere besides the cafeteria for lunch." He grinned suddenly. "I'll even buy. Deal?"

There seemed no escape. Adam hadn't said it—this time—but Liothel was sure, looking at him, that he would go to the police if she refused. "Deal," she said weakly.

"Good." Adam moved his arm. "Well, don't just stand there—you're going to be late for class!" He turned and trotted down the hall.

Liothel got through the morning relying heavily on an axiom that seemed common to both worlds: if you kept your head down so you didn't meet the teacher's eye (but not so low you appeared asleep), and never raised your hand, you would rarely, if ever, be called on to answer a question. Maribeth's memories didn't help her deal with the intricacies of the strange magic known as algebra; it seemed it was about as much of a mystery to Maribeth as it was to her.

143

Having felt that way in one or two of her own classes over the years, Liothel identified strongly with her host—and felt a pang yet again as she remembered what she, as Maribeth, intended to do. *Creator, there's got to be another way!* she cried in her heart, but knew, barring the miraculous appearance of an Exorcist, there was not.

True to his word, Adam awaited her when she emerged from the algebra classroom. "Whew—getting serious," Ellen whispered to her as she passed, then winked at Adam before giggling down the corridor in the company of Crystal.

Adam blinked after them, then turned to Liothel. "Ready?"

She sighed. "I guess so."

"McDonald's all right?"

She checked Maribeth's memories. "Sure."

"Let's go."

Adam said nothing in the Mustang, or in the restaurant, until they had taken their Big Macs and fries to a corner table. Enveloped in the McDonaldland din, there seemed little chance of anyone overhearing them. Adam unwrapped his hamburger and said, "All right, I've waited as long as I can. Give. What's going on? Why did your old 'friend' and her stupid gang try to kill us? Just because I stopped them hassling you?"

Liothel had decided to tell him as much of the truth as she thought he would believe—which wasn't much. "I think that's why you were included—but I think you were just bait. They really wanted me."

"Oh, come on. What could you have done to make a bunch of jerks like that want to kill you?" He frowned. "Hey, you're not mixed up with drugs or anything like that, are you?"

Was she? Maribeth's memories were blank on the subject, except for a well-hidden, experimental, and thoroughly disgusting puff on some noxious weed rolled into a cylinder and set alight. "No, of course not. Look, you arrived in town after the accident Mari—I was in last semester, didn't you?"

He nodded. "The first I even knew you existed was the day they announced you had woken up. Everybody was talking about it." He took a bite of his Big Mac, then wiped a stray bit of sauce from his mouth. "So?"

"So didn't anyone mention Christine Redpath was also in that accident?"

He stared at her. "You're kidding."

"No." Liothel picked up a french fry, then put it down again without taking a bite.

"Then why does she want to kill you?"

For the same reason I may have to kill her, Liothel thought. "Something—happened to her," she said slowly. "Something—in her head." That was true enough. From what Maribeth had learned, Christine had changed right after the accident. Not because of the soulworm; it had only been in her for a few weeks—it had just taken advantage of what it had found. But however mentally messed up Christine had been because of the accident, it hadn't made a killer out of her. That was entirely the soulworm's work. And even so, Maribeth was the target only because of Liothel's presence.

Liothel had no appetite for the overcooked food before her. She pushed it away. "I think maybe she blames me for—for Tom."

"Tom?"

"Her boyfriend. He died in the crash."

"Oh!" Adam looked like he wished he hadn't eaten a bite of his hamburger, either. "I'm sorry, I didn't—"

"It's all right." Liothel cleared her throat. Here was where she and the truth parted company. "Anyway, that's

145

why I don't want you to go to the police. I want to talk to Christine first, see if—I don't know, if I can bring her around. If the police find out she had anything to do with that fire, they'll charge her with arson, and maybe attempted murder—and maybe put her away as criminally insane, but that's even worse. I just can't help thinking that if I can talk to her, alone..."

"Not alone."

"Adam, I can't let you—"

"I can't let you talk to her alone," he said stubbornly. "You just said she may be crazy and she definitely wants to kill you. You think those punks she calls a gang wouldn't do it? I know their kind. You get enough of them together, and they'll do anything just to prove they're scummier than their buddies. And I don't know how, but she's got them wrapped around her little finger—" A shadow fell across the table, and they both looked up, blinking—into the eyes of Christine.

Vision blurred for Liothel, and sharper than Maribeth had ever seen it, she saw the bloody fire wreathing Christine's form, the soulworm writhing within her like some scaly, deadly serpent trapped beneath her skin. She shuddered and shrank away.

"How nice to see both of you looking so well." Christine's voice dripped venom.

Adam stood, jaw working. "Beat it, Christine."

One of the bulkier Ice Devils appeared behind him and gripped his shoulder in a leather-gloved hand. "You keep out of this, Metcalfe." The Devil grinned nastily. "How's your head? Nasty cut you've got there."

"You son of a—unnh!" Adam winced as the Ice Devil's fingers tightened.

"You can't do anything here," Liothel said, speaking not only to Christine but to the soulworm hiding inside. "There are too many people."

"Do? I just came over to say hello."

But Liothel's fingers tightened spasmodically on the edge of the table, for underneath Christine's voice she heard, *"I Will Kill Her Kill Her Kill Her But Not Here Not Now It's Too Soon Four More Days Is All And The Pain The Pleasure The Spawning She Can't Stop Me Nothing Can Stop Me This World Will Be Mine/ours—no! She Hears!"*

The undercurrent of strange words faded like a voice moving away, but somehow Liothel knew she could have pursued it, focused on it, followed it down into Christine's mind. In shock she let it go, and swayed, heart pounding.

Christine's eyes suddenly blazed with fresh hatred. "Let him go!" she snapped at the Ice Devil, then leaned over and said to Liothel, in a voice soft but sharp as a sword, "We'll get together again real soon, Maribeth. Real, real soon." Then she spun and strode away.

Adam stared after her, then turned on Liothel. "You want to talk to *that*? Maribeth, you've got to go to the police! You've got to!"

Liothel hardly heard him, lost in a swirling haze of mingled elation, hope and fear.

She had seen the soulworm's sign, as she had expected—but then she had heard its thoughts. And that was no ability of a Detector; that was one of the Gifts of the Exorcist.

She was both! Like Jara, who had been meant for this task, she was dual-talented. She had the ability to drive the soulworm out of Christine without killing her, without making Maribeth a murderer.

Therein lay elation and hope, but at their centre was a dark core of fear, the fear of failure that had dogged her all

147

those years as an Acolyte, bolstered this time by one stark truth—she had the ability of an Exorcist, but no training. And one thing she knew about Exorcists:

Those who failed, died.

19

The Appointment

"Maribeth? Maribeth, do you hear me? You've got to go to the police!"

As though surfacing from a great depth of dark water, Liothel's consciousness returned to the noise and light of McDonald's. She looked around. It seemed wrong, terribly wrong, that this bright, cheerful place should remain unchanged after that unspeakable thing had been standing right there....

"No," she said, finally reacting to what Adam had said. "No police. I told you, I want to talk to her first."

"You just did. She threatened you. I heard her. And with the Ice Devils to back her up, she can do whatever she wants to you. You can't stop her. The police—"

"The police can't do anything until she actually does something," Liothel said, calling on Maribeth's knowledge again.

"But she threatened you—"

"Not in so many words." Liothel looked down at her still-untouched food and pushed it away, nauseated. "Adam, I don't like this any better than you do. But I still think the only hope is if I can...talk...to Christine."

Adam glared at her; she returned his gaze steadily, and finally it softened. "All right," he said. "All right!" He leaned forward and pointed at her. "But you listen to me. You're not talking to her alone, and you're not talking to

149

her in private. It's got to be a public place, and I have to be close by."

"She won't talk if you can overhear her."

"I don't have to hear what you say, but I'm sure as hell going to see you say it. You're playing with fire, Maribeth."

Liothel laughed shakily. "Don't remind me."

Adam looked puzzled, then smiled a little. "Pun unintentional." He stood up and dumped their trays through the swinging door of the garbage bin. "Come on, let's get out of here. It's almost time for class."

During the ride back to school Liothel thought about what Adam had said, and decided it made no difference whether he was there or not. The "talk" she planned with Christine was only a step toward the final confrontation, not the exorcism itself. She only hoped to get more information. And if letting Adam hover nearby was the only way to keep him from going to the police and bringing things to a head too soon...

"The rink."

"What?" Adam glanced at her.

"That's where I'll meet her—at the Colosseum. During public skating. She won't try anything there. And you can watch us from almost anywhere in the building."

He nodded slowly. "Okay. If I can't talk you out of it—"

"You can't."

"Then that will have to do." He turned off King Street and pulled up in front of the school. "You just tell me when—if you can get her to meet you there. Which I doubt. Her idea of an ideal meeting place would be a dark alley."

"She'll meet me." Liothel knew it was true; now that the soulworm knew that the Warder in Maribeth was in full control, it must be as anxious for more knowledge about its

150

adversary as she was. They would be feeling each other out like swordsmen, looking for weaknesses.

Liothel only hoped hers were not as glaring as they felt.

Arranging the meeting proved easier than she had dreamed. Christine, apparently on the spur of the moment, was back in school, sitting glassy-eyed in classes and during breaks holding court on a bench near the glass doors of the library. The Ice Devils clustered around her like a pack of wild dogs.

Liothel, accompanied by Crystal and Ellen, emerged from a side corridor. Her friends grabbed her arms and pulled her to a stop when they saw the group by the library, halfway down the hall.

"Let's...take the long way around," Ellen said.

"The longer the better," agreed Crystal.

"You go on," Liothel said, as Christine stiffened and turned to look at her. "I have to talk to Christine."

Ellen and Crystal exchanged glances. "Oh...we're in no hurry."

"Yeah," said Crystal. "We'll wait for you. Right here." She let go of Liothel's arm. "But don't be long."

Liothel nodded, all her attention on Christine and the Ice Devils. She started toward them, step by slow step. Other students hurried past, all giving the Ice Devils a wide berth, but Liothel hardly saw them. Only Christine's face, half-smiling, mocking, was clear—clear but distant, as though at the end of a long tunnel.

Then suddenly she was right in front of Maribeth's old friend, and everything snapped back to normal.

The Devils stood in unison; Rick took half a step toward her, but stopped at a glance from Christine. The look he gave Christine in return sickened Liothel; it was almost mindless, and in Maribeth's memories, Rick, while hardly one of her favorite people, had never been anyone's crony.

151

The power of the soulworm was growing, Liothel realized; its hold on those who would be the first hosts for the second generation was strengthening. It was building a nest, though such an image of domestic tranquility seemed obscene when applied to this horror.

"Quite a surprise, Maribeth," Christine said. "I don't remember asking you over."

"We have to talk." Liothel kept her voice as steady as she could. "Alone."

"Oh, you don't need to worry about the Ice Devils," said Christine. "Their lips are sealed...except when I want them open. If you know what I mean."

"Alone," Liothel repeated. "Unless you're afraid."

"Afraid? Of you?"

"Well, if you won't even talk..."

"I never said I wouldn't talk to you. I just don't see the point." But her eyes narrowed, and Liothel knew she—or the soulworm—was considering the possibilities. "Where?"

"The Colosseum. There's public skating at seven-thirty."

Christine laughed. "Who's scared? You want as many people around as possible."

"Will you be there?"

"Yeah, sure, why not? It'll kill a few minutes." But then she leaned forward and looked straight into Liothel's eyes, and for an instant the soulworm shone through full-force, the evil glow of its power oozing from Christine's body, and that horrible voice she had heard at McDonald's echoed inside her head, though Christine's lips never moved. *But Our Next Meeting Will Be When And Where I Choose, And Be Assured—at That Meeting, We Will Kill More Than Time.*

Liothel hoped her borrowed face didn't betray her inner trembling as she said, "See you at seven-thirty, then," and turned and walked away, feeling Christine's gaze like an icy wind at her back.

"What happened?" Ellen demanded as she and Crystal hurried along the corridor—not the one where the Ice Devils lurked—with Liothel between them. "What did she say?"

"We're going skating," Liothel said, and left them staring after her outside her classroom door.

Adam said nothing later in the day when she told him of her appointment with Christine—only grunted and hurried to his next class. Liothel looked after him. He's really worried about me, she thought, pleased...then remembered that she wasn't who he thought she was, and turned away, confused.

Her plan had one tiny flaw in it that she didn't discover until that evening at supper. "There's one thing about being grounded," Maribeth's father said cheerfully as he put salad on her plate. "You'll have plenty of time to catch up on all that schoolwork you missed."

Grounded! Liothel had forgotten. Frantically she racked Maribeth's memories for the rules of being grounded—and groaned inside. Skating was definitely not on the list of permissible activities.

She opened her mouth to ask permission—then closed it again. Better not to warn them, she thought. I'll sneak out. Maybe they won't miss me, if they think I'm upstairs doing homework....

But as she picked at her food and listened to Maribeth's parents joke and laugh with Sean, she felt dirty and dishonest. They loved their daughter so much, and Liothel had put her in danger just by being there...and would put her in even more danger over the next few days. It was small comfort that Maribeth would not have to become a murderer when she might still become a victim.

And Liothel hated lying. She looked across the table at Maribeth's father, so strong and full of life, yet tender, too, as she knew from Maribeth's memories. Those memories were the closest Liothel would ever come to having a father—those memories, and these few days when she was in Maribeth's body. But though she would have given anything in her own life to have a father just like him, she was going to have to break his heart.

Maribeth's mother said something and Liothel looked at her, too, remembering long, heart-to-heart talks between mother and daughter and other special times together. Liothel loved Jara, but it wasn't the same....

"Maribeth, you're really in another world tonight," Maribeth's father remarked, and she jumped. "If I may repeat myself, please pass the butter."

She handed it over, then asked to be excused.

At a quarter after seven she crept down the stairs, listening to canned television laughter from the living room and the quick clacking of computer keys in Mrs. Gayle's study. If she were lucky, both Sean and his father would be so engrossed in whatever was on—she heard them laughing together, Mr. Gayle's deep voice in counterpoint to Sean's childish one—that they wouldn't notice her during that brief moment she would be in sight at the bottom of the stairs. Then as long as Miser didn't bark...

For a moment she thought she had done it. Mr. Gayle, just visible in the living room, didn't look up, and she was quickly out of his sight. But as she put her hand on the front door latch, Sean emerged, heading for the kitchen, and blurted, "Hey, Maribeth, where are you going?"

Liothel shot him one anguished look, then jerked the door open and fled, hearing Maribeth's father calling after her.

20

The Dark Plain

Liothel ran down the quiet street where Maribeth lived to busy (for Weyburn) First Avenue, then followed it south, paralleling the high chain-link fence enclosing the fairgrounds. On the other side of the grandstand she could see the lights of the Colosseum, and hear the roar of its ventilation system, spewing out great clouds of vapor that shimmered in the moonlight, as though a great dragon grew restless in the night.

But the sound that lingered in her mind was that of Maribeth's father calling his daughter's name. Liothel was going to meet the terrible creature she was sworn to destroy, but all she could think about was how she had hurt Maribeth's parents—and Maribeth, too, wherever she was.

As she followed the alley at the south end of the fairgrounds to the Colosseum's parking lot, though, and saw Christine's white Camaro parked beneath a streetlight, she tried to thrust the problems she was creating in Maribeth's family out of her mind. She had only the vaguest idea of what to expect; she would need all her concentration if she were to get any useful information without risking too much.

Just as she turned toward the Colosseum's entrance, she glimpsed Adam's Mustang, half-hidden by a snow-covered hedge. Relief, however unreasonable, swept through her. Though she knew Adam had no idea of the truth, and couldn't do anything to help even if he did, still it was comforting to know that he cared enough to—

Cares enough about Maribeth, some inner voice spoke up cruelly. *He doesn't even know you exist.*

She banged the door open with rather more force than was necessary.

She hadn't specified where in the Colosseum she would meet Christine; she stood just inside and slowly scanned the sparse crowd in the lobby, mostly parents busy tying or untying their children's skates, zipping or unzipping their children's coats, gossiping with one another while sipping cups of steaming coffee, or staring numbly out the windows at the ice surface, acrawl with skaters ranging from wobbly toddlers to one slow but graceful elderly couple.

But on or off the ice there was no sign of her enemy. She circled the lobby, frowning, then went out into the stands and peered through the curving Plexiglas puck screen at the skaters. She still couldn't see...

Something pricked her consciousness like a needle, a small sense of not-quite-right. She looked up, up, from the ice to the stands to the press box just under the arching roof; and there she saw Christine, looking down at her, and for a moment the other girl's eyes seemed to flash red fire.

Liothel took a deep breath and crossed behind the end boards, then mounted the stairs, feeling Christine's gaze on her until she reached the very top, out of the press box's line-of-sight. From there she glanced back down, and saw Adam standing beneath the goal-judge's chair, watching her. She waved, but he didn't wave back; only followed her with his eyes as she walked across the top row of the stands to the door of the press box.

She stepped through into the tiny, glass-enclosed room, with its long, scarred wooden desk punctuated by empty microphone stands. It smelled of stale cigarette smoke. Christine sat in one of four battered gray metal chairs, looking down at the ice, and said, without turning around, "About time you got here."

"I didn't know you were on a tight schedule." Out of the corner of her eye she saw Adam starting up the stands. Christine wasn't looking at him, but to distract her, Liothel said quickly, "I wanted to talk to you. I thought, if we could talk..."

"If we could talk, we could work out all our differences?" Suddenly Christine surged out of her chair, grabbing Liothel's wrists and smashing her back against the wall. "YOU'RE A FOOL, WARDER," came the soulworm's silent, mocking voice. "*You Cannot Stop My Host By Talk; You Cannot Stop Me By Action. you Have Not The Knowledge For The First Or The Skill For The Second. the Warders Have Tormented My Kind For Centuries In Our World, But Here—here, There Are No Warders. here, We Will Thrive. here, I And My Offspring Will Rule!*" The fiery glow of the soulworm filled Liothel's vision, obliterating Christine's features, and the press box faded around them, giving way to an infinite plain of jet black, beneath a mist-grey sky. "*Welcome To The Dark Field—the Field Of Battle! you Are Untrained And Weak, And I Am Only Three Days From Spawning. here You Die, Warder. here, And Now!*"

Christine's appearance changed, running like wax, swelling and twisting until no human semblance was left, and in her place towered a hideous dragon. Scales clanked like plates of steel, fire hissed and popped, acid dripped from claws like ivory tusks. High above Liothel's head the creature loomed, waves of withering heat emanating from it, while she stood powerless, frozen with fear and uncertainty. *Is this real, or illusion?* she wondered. *Can it really hurt me, or—*

And then she screamed as the dragon plunged to the attack, mouth gaping to swallow her whole.

But before those mighty teeth closed, the creature vanished. Liothel reeled as reality collided with her senses. Christine, eyes raging with the soulworm's fire, picked herself up from the floor of the press box, while Adam stood over her with clenched fists. "You keep your hands off her," he snarled, "or by God—"

Christine spat a string of obscenities, but over or beneath them Liothel heard the soulworm. "*And In Time He, Too, Will Be Mine! you Have Won No Victory—Only A Stay Of Execution!*" And then Christine fled the press box.

Liothel slumped against the desk, and Adam knelt beside her. "Are you all right?" He helped her into a chair. "What happened?"

Liothel hardly heard him, and when she spoke it was to herself. "She's strong," she whispered. "So strong...I didn't know what to do. I was so scared...she could have killed me, if not for—" She focused on Adam. "You saved my life."

He looked away. "Oh, she wouldn't have done anything too serious, not here...but you've seen what she's like. Now will you go to the police?"

"No." Liothel pushed sweaty strands of hair back from her forehead. "There's no time. There's only three days until..." She broke off.

"Until what?"

"Nothing." Liothel tried to get up, but her knees were too weak and she sank back into the chair.

Adam glared at her. "Look, Maribeth, I gave you your chance to talk to her. Now we try it my way. I'm going to the police!"

"Adam, no!" Liothel grabbed his arm. "Please! You don't know what—"

"Then tell me!" he shouted, jerking free. "Maribeth, I'm trying to help you, but you're making it impossible!"

158

"I can't tell you!" Liothel cried. "You'd never believe me!"

"At least give me the chance! After everything that's happened, you owe me that much!"

"I—" Liothel could get no further around the lump in her throat. The Creator knew she wanted to tell Adam—wanted to tell him everything—not just about the soulworm and the Warders but about herself, her life, so he would know she was Liothel and not Maribeth, so that the light that sometimes came in his eyes when he looked at Maribeth might be for her. But it was so terribly impossible that it hurt like a vise crushing her heart. He would not believe her; he could not, in this world. The only conclusion he could draw would be that Maribeth had gone crazy. He'd tell her parents, and there'd be doctors and hospitals and endless tests for Maribeth...and for Liothel, the dreadful knowledge that she had failed the Warders just as she had always feared she would, that the soulworm had spawned freely, and that the violence that was both the soulworm's food and excrement would spread like a plague through even this most peaceful part of the Earth.

Almost roughly, Adam seized her hands, looked into her eyes. "Maribeth, please! Please trust me. Nothing could be so bad that you couldn't share it with me. I want to help you so much..." And then he gave a final twist to the vise gripping her heart: "I love you."

"No!" Liothel tore her hands free. "You don't! You can't! You don't even know who I am—"

She tried to get up, to run past him, but he grabbed her and held her down, though she writhed in his grip. "Maribeth, stop it! Stop it!" She subsided, but kept her face turned away. Hot tears blinded her. Below them, the incongruous strains of "The Skater's Waltz" floated over the ice.

"Maybe I don't know who you are," Adam said, his voice low and intense. "I haven't known you long enough. But everything I do know makes me want to know more. Maybe I shouldn't say I love you until I do know more about you. Maybe you can't really love someone you've only known for a few days. But if I don't love you, Maribeth, then believe me, I'm working on it. There's something about you, I—" His voice broke off. "Hell, I sound like a soap opera. Look, Maribeth, my head's so mixed up I don't know what I feel. But I can't stand the thought of anything happening to you, and I'll do anything I can to stop it. Maybe that's not love, but it's still got to count for something." He paused. "Won't you at least look at me?"

Slowly Liothel turned her head. Adam's face was only inches from her own. She looked into his blue eyes, and for a disconcerting moment slipped inside them—inside his mind, bright and free of any taint of the soulworm, filled at the moment with one overwhelming urge —

—to kiss her.

His lips were on hers (Maribeth's) hers (Maribeth's) hers hers hers—

The passion of the moment gave way to sudden horror. Maribeth's body still responded, but Liothel's mind recoiled. She was a Warder, she had sworn an oath of celibacy—she was endangering her powers, the powers she had to have to defeat the soulworm—she had to...had to...

What she had to do faded in another surge of desire generated by the body she wore, but brutally, coldly, she stamped across her mind an image of the soulworm as a dragon, towering over her, and pushed Adam away.

"Wha—" He stared at her, breathing hard, and licked his lips. "What's wrong?"

"I've got to leave now." Liothel tried to sound firm, but her traitorous voice trembled. "I can't—I've got to go home."

"I'll walk you." Adam took her hand and she closed her eyes against the surging need to hold him tight.

"No," she whispered, and pulled free.

"Maribeth—"

"Adam, I—" Her voice broke. "I just can't, right now. Not until this thing with Christine is over. I—I can't. Do you understand?"

"No, I don't! This is the second time this has happened. I kiss you, and you—"

"The second time?" Liothel searched those hazy memories from before the fire, found what he was referring to. Even that she had messed up for Maribeth; it must have been some leakage of her own vows that had caused Maribeth to recoil so violently at the door after her first date with Adam. "Adam, I'm sorry, it's just that I've got so much on my mind—"

"Well, I wish you'd share a little of it. You still haven't told me anything, and after what I saw in here tonight, I still think—"

"Please!" She reached out involuntarily, pulled her hand back before she touched him. "Please. No police. Three days. Three days, that's all I need. Three days, and all of this will be over. Then..."

"Then?"

I wish I knew, Liothel thought miserably. *Creator, how I wish I knew.* "Promise me three days?"

Adam took a deep breath and spoke as though words were being squeezed out of him. "I promise." Liothel knew she was hurting him—hurting him like she had hurt everyone she had come in contact with in this world. *Warders aren't supposed to hurt people!* she cried silently. *Jara, what am I doing wrong?*

Adam must have seen something of her turmoil in her face. "Maribeth—" He steppd toward her.

She backed away. "Thank you," she whispered, then stumbled out of the press box and down the stands. At the lobby door she stopped and looked back, and saw Adam still watching her from the press box.

It took all her willpower to turn and leave him behind.

21

To Tell
The Truth

And then, of course, she had to face Maribeth's parents.

They were waiting for her. Sean was nowhere to be seen; always an ominous sign, Maribeth's memories told her. She wished she could just walk past them, go to her room and try to sort out what she had to do next, but she knew that would only make matters worse.

In any event, Maribeth's father heard her come in and blocked her path. "In here," he said, and she followed him into the living room. He sat in the big, burnt-umber reclining armchair and Maribeth's mother sat on the matching couch; all that left Liothel was the rather uncomfortable chair in the corner that faced away from the television and was therefore little used.

"We'd like an explanation," Mr. Gayle said when she was seated. "Where did you go?"

"To the Colosseum." Liothel was determined to be as truthful as possible, in the forlorn hope it would mitigate what she was doing to Maribeth's relationship with her parents.

"Why?"

"To meet someone."

"Who?"

Liothel hesitated. "Christine."

Mrs. Gayle's mouth tightened. Maribeth's father frowned. "Why did you have to see her tonight? And what was so urgent you went even though you were grounded?"

"We've had some...arguments. I hoped if we talked about them, we could—work things out."

"I don't like you seeing her," Maribeth's mother broke in. "I told you that. She's not the same."

"No," Liothel said quietly. "She's not."

"Neither are you," said Maribeth's father, his face stern. "You've never defied us like this before."

"Defied?" Liothel stared at him. "But I didn't—I admit I disobeyed you, but—"

"You didn't just disobey! You sneaked out of the house and kept running while I called after you. We had no idea when you were coming home—or if you were coming home—where you were, or who you were with."

"I'm sorry. I should have left a note—"

"You shouldn't have gone at all! But even worse than disobeying us, you didn't trust us. Don't you think you could have talked to us about your problems with Christine? If it was really so important to meet her tonight, you should have told us. We would have understood. We might even have given you permission."

Liothel opened her mouth, closed it again. "I didn't think of that."

"Was Christine the only one you met?" asked Mrs. Gayle.

Liothel wondered how she had guessed. "No," she said, a little reluctantly, because she didn't want to talk about it. "No, Adam was there, too. He was afraid Christine might—do something. He wanted to protect me."

"I thought as much. That's twice he's gotten you in trouble, and you've only known him a week."

"He didn't—"

"He was there."

Liothel kept quiet, sensing that further argument would be counterproductive.

"Your mother and I have decided to extend your grounding for two weeks," Maribeth's father said, getting to his feet. "And until it is over, we want you to stay away from Adam Metcalfe. You can talk to him at school, but I don't want to hear you talking to him on the phone or see him bringing you home from anywhere or taking you to McDonald's for lunch. Understood?" He waited until Liothel nodded, then stalked out.

Maribeth's mother also stood, but came over to Liothel and touched her cheek. "We love you," she said softly. "But we're worried about you. You're...changing."

Not knowing what to say, Liothel looked down. Mrs. Gayle kissed her on the forehead, then followed her husband upstairs.

Liothel went up, too, though it was still too early to go to sleep, and lay on her stomach on the bed, resting her chin on the blue-frilled pillow and staring at the glowing green numbers of the clock radio on the headboard. Downstairs the television came on again as Sean sensed the coast was clear.

She needed to think about exorcising and destroying the soulworm, but her thoughts kept drifting to Maribeth and her parents. They didn't understand what had happened to their daughter, and she couldn't tell them. She didn't even know where Maribeth was, not really. Somewhere inside this body her spirit lingered, but it was hiding, hiding from something even Liothel did not understand, something to do with fire and Christine. She only hoped it wasn't something she might need to know before the end.

The end. That was coming far too quickly. She closed her eyes, seeing again the soulworm on that ebony plain, fiery dragon-jaws stretching to bite her in two. She hadn't done anything to fight back; she'd just stood there, mesmerized by the creature's power. "The battle of the Dark Plain." Jara had mentioned that more than once. Was that what she meant? But what could she have done? That was its realm, not hers.

Her eyes snapped open as something else Jara had said in one of her classes came back to her: "The soulworm has only a tenuous connection to what we call reality. It lives far more in the world of the spirit, the mind, the imagination. When it acts in the real world, it acts through its human host; outside a host, it is nothing but a wraith, vulnerable and easily destroyed. Therefore it will do everything in its power to stay in that netherworld where it is strong. To destroy a soulworm the Exorcist must go into that realm and wrest the soulworm from it, drive it out of the mind of its host and into reality, where the Warrior waits with the Circle of Fire."

Imagination, Liothel thought. *Illusion. It created the dragon from images in Christine's mind—and it grew stronger as I believed in it, believed I was really seeing the soulworm. I put myself in its power. I should have drawn on my own imagination, created my own illusion, discounted its image in favor of one of my own. It wanted me to see it as the hunter and me as the prey; but I have to make it see itself as prey. I have to make it flee—and then be ready to destroy it when it leaves Christine's body.*

Until that moment she hadn't thought that far; but now she realized with a sinking feeling that she couldn't do it alone, though perhaps Jara could have. She would have to have help, someone to play the role of Warrior, to build the Circle of Fire....

"Adam," she whispered, in the face of her own denial. It would have to be Adam. There simply was no one else. But how could she convince him to do what must be done?

Maybe she should tell him the truth. Maybe he would believe her. He said he loved her....

He loves Maribeth.

He doesn't even know Maribeth. He's only spent one evening with her...the rest of the time he's been with me.

In Maribeth's body.

There's more there than physical attraction. There's got to be! Liothel told herself fiercely. *If it was just physical, he could have any one of a dozen girls in the school. There has to be something that's drawing the rest of him—and part of that has to be me. He's never known Maribeth when I wasn't a part of her. Even when she was here, I was influencing her. If I could make him understand that...*

He'll think Maribeth has gone crazy, the more cynical part of her argued again. *That's all. He'll think she has...* "multiple personalities," Maribeth's memories supplied. *He'll tell her parents—and he'll go to the police about Christine. He won't give you the three days.*

But if he loves me/her...

Maybe he would help her without knowing why. He wouldn't have to know exactly what was happening, only what she needed done. Surely he would trust her that little bit more. He had to! Time was short. Three days...she had learned that much, at least. But that knowledge was of little use by itself. She had to find out exactly where and how the soulworm planned to trigger the violence it needed for its spawning frenzy.

And for that, too, she could use Adam's help.

But for all the uncertainties inherent in her vague plan of action, for all her worries about Adam, what bothered her most later that evening as she lay sleepless in bed was that once again she would have to hurt Maribeth's family, and break the rules Maribeth's parents had laid down out of love.

The Ice Devils' cars were back at their usual place the next morning, headed by Christine's Camaro, but their drivers were not in sight. Through the day Liothel saw Christine only once; as she crossed a corridor, she felt that same pricking sense of discomfort she had felt in the Colosseum, and glanced the length of the hallway to see Christine lounging against the wall at the far end. Their eyes met, and even across eighty feet Liothel felt the soulworm's hatred. She shuddered and hurried out of sight.

She was more interested in seeing Adam, but despite looking for him all day, she didn't spot him until after the final bell. He was walking away from her down the hallway leading to the front door, and she ran to catch up to him. "Adam." He didn't turn around. "Adam!" She caught his arm.

He stopped, the muscles in his arm hard and tight as steel cords under her touch, and looked down at her. "Your three days aren't up yet."

"Adam, I need your help."

"You're ready to go to the police?"

"No!" She glanced around. "Look, let's find someplace else to talk. I don't want anyone to see us."

He looked toward the exit for a moment, then shrugged irritably and led the way to the nearest classroom. He closed the door, then sat on top of a desk and folded his arms. "So, talk."

"Christine is planning something." Liothel's words tumbled out. "Something dangerous, violent—something with the Ice Devils. It's going to happen before the end of the week. I need to know what it is."

"Why? So you can sell tickets?"

Liothel stared at him, stung. "What's wrong with you?"

"What's wrong with me?" He glared at her. "What's wrong with me?" He hopped off the desk. "I'll tell you what's wrong with me! I spent all night trying to convince myself I was right to let you talk me out of going to the police. It's only three days, I told myself. I love her, I can give her three days.

"But you know what? This other voice kept coming back, telling me, 'If what you're feeling really is love, and even if it's just infatuation with a beautiful chick playing hard to get—'" Liothel blinked. "'—maybe you really ought to stop her from doing whatever it is she's doing, 'cause it looks like it's got a good chance of getting her killed!'" He sat down again and leaned forward, his eyes level with hers. "Look, Maribeth, here in Weyburn you aren't used to street gangs—but I grew up in Vancouver, and I've seen them before. Maybe this Christine was different, once—I can only take your word for that—but she's one bad bitch now. And she's got those muscleheads she calls the Ice Devils wrapped around her finger. They've already tried to kill both of us, and they've threatened you over and over. You keep telling me to give it just a little more time. Well, Maribeth, whatever it is I'm feeling for you—and you've managed to confuse me pretty well on that score—you want to tell me why I should just stand by and watch you get yourself killed?"

Liothel opened her mouth; closed it again. So much for relying on his love to make him follow her blindly. It seemed she had a lot to learn about that emotion. "Adam, you don't understand how important it is. You've got to trust me—"

"Trust you? Why don't you try trusting me? If it's that important, tell me what's going on!"

His dark eyes bored into hers, until she had to look away; at once her gaze was caught by a large calendar on the bulletin board by the door. The dates of exams and assignments were marked with big red letters. The coming Friday was marked, "FINAL ASSIGNMENT DUE."

So is mine, she thought; but knew that if she failed, it wouldn't be her grade that would suffer, but this whole world—and as if that thought were too big to grasp, a small voice inside whispered, "and Acolytes for all the coming generations at Mykia will learn the story of how Liothel failed her vows..." and that hurt even more.

In one respect all her self-doubting fears were right: she was unworthy. She couldn't succeed on her own. She had to have help, and Adam was the only one who could provide that help. And he was right, too—it wasn't fair to ask him to follow her blindly, not when the stakes were so high and what must be done so dangerous.

He wouldn't believe her. How could he? Unless she could somehow prove it...

A possibility nudged her mind, and she recoiled from it. She couldn't—she wasn't a Sentinel—it wasn't right—

But if it worked, Adam would believe her.

He'd have to.

She licked dry lips, then turned back to Adam. "All right. This is the truth...."

22

Baiting The Trap

She had barely begun when Adam stopped her. "Wait a minute! What is this? It sounds like a bad paperback!"

"It's the truth. Isn't that what you wanted?"

"You expect me to believe this garbage?"

"I expect you to at least listen to me!" Liothel snapped, then regretted it. It seemed changing bodies hadn't done anything to ease the quick temper Jara and the other Warders had so often chastised her for. Adam stared at her, and she hurried on in a lower voice, "Just listen. Then say what you like."

With the air of humoring her, he leaned back and folded his arms. She pressed on, and this time he let her finish, though his mouth quirked with suppressed laughter.

"There," she said at last. "That's the whole story. Now do you see why I don't want you to go to the police?"

"Oh, sure." Adam chuckled. "That's a pretty good story. Now how about the real one?"

"That was the real one." She looked away. "I told you you wouldn't believe me."

"Well, you've got to admit it's just a little hard to swallow! Let me see if I've got this straight: you're not really Maribeth, you're a priestess from another world who has come here to destroy a demon that has possessed Christine. Is that about it?"

"Essentially."

"Oh, well, of course I should believe that!" Adam shook his head. "Just like I believe in Superman and the tooth fairy! Now come on, Maribeth, give me a break and give me the real story. You've had your joke. Write it down and you could probably sell it. But enough's enough."

"I wasn't joking. My name is Liothel, and I am a Warder of Mykia."

Adam frowned. "Maribeth, stop it! I'm beginning to think you actually believe this stuff."

Liothel took a deep breath. "I can prove it," she said, and hoped she was telling the truth.

"Oh, really?"

"Yes. I told you one of our skills is to detect the presence of a soulworm. But there's another aspect of that skill. Only when the soulworm is making no attempt to hide is it as easy as it has been for me with Christine. Often the soulworm is very well hidden, deep inside the host. To find it, we must look inside the host's mind, as deeply as necessary." She met Adam's eyes. "But it doesn't have to be someone possessed. I can look into anyone's mind—including yours."

"Are you telling me you can read my mind?"

"It happened last night, when you rescued me from Christine. I could feel what you felt. And I wasn't even trying."

"And just what was I feeling?"

Liothel looked away. "You wanted to kiss me."

"Brilliant, considering that's what I did. It's a shame you didn't feel the same way."

"Warders are sworn to celibacy. I couldn't—I can't afford those kind of—feelings. It could interfere with my ability to face the soulworm—"

"Oh, come on!" Adam jumped to his feet. "Maribeth, if you don't feel anything for me, just tell me. Don't use this stupid story as an excuse. And as for reading my mind—what's wrong with you, anyway? Christine wants to kill you and you want to show me magic tricks? Will you..."

His voice faded from Liothel's conscious mind as she closed her eyes, said a brief prayer to the Creator, then tried to do on purpose what she had done involuntarily the night before.

For a moment she felt helpless, unable to recapture that sense of falling into Adam's eyes. But suddenly it happened of its own accord, and with a wrenching sensation, her consciousness plunged into his.

...what's Wrong With Her Why Is She Looking Like That Has She Gone Nuts Is It Worth It Sure She's Good-looking But—what Is She Doing No It's Impossible She Really Is Reading My Mind She's Saying Every Word I Think Stop It Maribeth Stop It Stop It Stop It!...

The connection snapped and she opened her eyes to find Adam gripping her arms, shaking her. "Stop it! Stop it!"

"Adam, you're hurting me," she whispered. Her throat had gone dry.

He let go and backed away from her, wild-eyed. "You were reading my mind! You really were reading my mind!"

She nodded.

"Everything I thought, you repeated, perfectly, word for word..." He kept backing away, down the aisle between the desks, until his back was pressed against the blackboard. "Maribeth, what's going on?"

Liothel sighed. She felt very tired. "I told you. I'm not Maribeth."

He stared at her. "It's true, isn't it?" he whispered. "Everything you told me—it's true!"

"It is."

173

He slid down the wall until he was sitting on the brown-flecked tiles on the floor, his back to the pale blue cinder blocks.

Liothel went to him, and he drew his knees up tight against his chest as she approached. "Please, Adam, don't be afraid of me," she said, sitting cross-legged on the floor in front of him.

"I'm not," he insisted; then smiled weakly. "Well, not much, anyway. But it's creepy to know you know what I'm thinking."

"I don't! Really, I don't! Only when I try hard, like I did a few minutes ago. And the way I feel," she added, "I don't particularly want to try again anytime soon."

"Good." Adam looked at her, curiousity replacing shock. "What did you say your name is?"

"Liothel." Liothel smiled at him. "No last name. We don't use them."

"Liothel," Adam repeated. "It's a nice name."

"Thank you." The compliment warmed her disproportionately.

Adam took a deep breath. "So, Liothel. You've talked me out of going to the police..."

"I thought you might decide against that."

Adam laughed a little. "I'd still like to, but this soulworm thing doesn't sound like something you can put in prison."

"One of your prisons," Liothel said on the strength of Maribeth-knowledge of riots and killings, "would be the worst possible place we could send it. It would spawn wildly there. The only thing that has given me time to even hope to stop it has been the fact that the Gate opened into this small city. It's having to generate its own violence. That's why, using Christine, it has formed the Ice Devils. But it's almost ready, now. Whatever it has planned will happen in the next couple of days. I learned that much last night—just before you rescued me."

"If I'd known all this then, I'd have probably been too scared to do anything," Adam muttered.

"No!" Liothel reached out and touched his knee, so that he raised his eyes to her. "I don't believe that!"

For a moment they stared at each other; then she pulled her hand back and cleared her throat. "Anyway, what I have to find out now is what Christine has planned, and when and where it will happen. That's where I need your help. I need you to listen in the halls, in the locker rooms, anywhere you might hear some clue. I'll do the same."

"I seriously doubt the Ice Devils are talking. Not the way Christine has them under her thumb."

"You may be right," Liothel admitted. "But if we don't find out anything this way, I think I know someone I can convince to tell me."

"Who?"

She looked away. "I'd rather not say."

"Supposing we do find out what's planned. What then?"

"Then you're going to have to have a crash course in being a Warrior of Wardfast Mykia."

"We've only got two days."

"I know," Liothel said softly. "Believe me, I know."

The next day Liothel listened, and asked subtle and not-so-subtle questions, and learned absolutely nothing. The Ice Devils weren't telling anyone anything; or if they were, those they told knew better in turn than to open their mouths. Liothel met Adam the next afternoon in the same classroom.

"Well?" she asked him as he came in.

"Nothing. Nobody's heard a thing." Disappointed, Liothel sat at one of the desks. Adam sat on top of it. "Are you sure about this?"

"Yes." She picked at her sweater with one hand. "I guess I'm going to have to go to my last-chance source."

Adam gave her a sharp look. "I don't like the sound of that."

Liothel jumped up. "I'll see you tomorrow." She hurried out, feeling Adam staring after her.

After supper she dialed the phone in her room. The line rang six times before a woman answered, her voice thin and harsh against a background of blaring TV laughter. "Yeah?"

"May I speak to Rick?"

"He's not here." The woman yelled, "Turn that thing down, will you? Can't you see I'm on the phone?" then spoke to Liothel again. "He's off somewhere with his hooligan friends. He always is."

"Well, can I leave a message?"

"Yeah, sure, just a minute..." There was a clatter as the phone was put down; then, above the still-loud TV, Liothel heard a door open and close, and the woman shouted, "Hey, Rick! Phone!"

Someone picked up the phone and a sullen voice asked, "Who is it?"

Liothel's heart pounded from Maribeth's memories of that voice. But she said as coolly as she could, "Rick, this is Maribeth Gayle."

His voice roughened. "Yeah? What do you want?"

"I want to apologize."

"Huh?"

"For the other day, by the lockers...and the time before that. I was just being...immature."

"I don't—"

"I'd really like for us to get together again, Rick," Liothel purred, feeling dirty. "Maybe we could finish what we started."

Silence on the other end, except for breathing and the TV. "Yeah," Rick said finally. "I'd like that. When?"

"Why not tonight? Late. Say, 10:30. Pick me up at the 7-11."

"You got it." Liothel could almost see his leer. "Little girl, you're in for the night of your life."

Liothel swallowed. "I'm sure I am. I'll see you later. 'Bye."

"Not for long, girl. Not for long."

The moment she had hung up Liothel curled herself into a ball on the bed and hugged her knees tight to her chest, trying to stop shaking. *Maribeth, I'm sorry!* she cried in her heart. *I'll do my best to keep us both safe—but I have to know what the Ice Devils are up to. I have to!*

Does that give you the right to use her body as bait? an inner voice snarled. *Who are you to play Creator? You're no better than the soulworm!*

Maribeth would help me if I could ask her. I know she would!

But in fact Liothel didn't know; couldn't know. She had the other girl's memories, but her personality, her soul, was hidden somewhere out of sight. Liothel only hoped that when, and if, Maribeth returned to claim her body, she would still have a life worth living.

If anything goes wrong, the inner voice pointed out, *she won't have a life at all.*

Neither will I, Liothel thought, and hugged herself tighter.

23

Rick

There was no drama later that night when Liothel sneaked out of the house to meet Rick at the 7-11; no one saw her, no one heard her, no one stood in the doorway shouting after her. But still she ran down the icy sidewalk, as though by hurrying she could leave behind the mess she knew she was making of Maribeth's relationship with her parents.

Maybe it's just as well I never knew mine, she thought as she finally turned the corner onto First Avenue and left the accusing gleam of the house's windows behind her. *I don't seem to be very good at getting along with them.*

The 7-11 was just a few blocks from the Gayles' house, built in a prime location at the intersection of First Avenue and Government Road, not far from the school. Liothel's heart beat faster and faster as she approached it. What if Rick had told the other Ice Devils? What if he had told Christine? She could be precipitating a showdown she wasn't prepared for—a battle she was sure to lose.

But when the 7-11 parking lot finally came into sight, there was only one Firebird in it—Rick's, which she knew all too well from Maribeth's unpleasant memories of the night she had started out riding in the car and ended up walking home. Somehow, seeing it did little to ease her apprehension.

In fact, her heart beat even harder.

The big black car crouched at the very edge of the parking lot, its exhaust wreathing it in drifting vapor. As Liothel took her first step onto the concrete the driver's door opened and Rick emerged from a white cloud of steam, his dark form for a moment seeming forbidding, larger than life, then shrinking to his own average build, red hair, leather jacket and lewd grin. "I knew you'd change your mind," he said. "I've got what you want."

Liothel forced herself to smile. "When you're right, you're right."

"Get in." He climbed back into the driver's seat, unlatched the passenger door from inside and pushed it open. Liothel rounded the spoilered rear of the car and slid into the form-fitting seat, the white fur that covered it seeming to embrace her. She barely got the door closed before Rick gunned the engine and shot out of the parking lot backward, slewing to a stop in the highway and then accelerating away toward the edge of town.

"Where are we going?" Liothel said. Her mouth was so dry it was hard to talk.

Rick grinned at her. "Didn't you say you wanted to finish what we started?

"Oh..." She should have guessed.

She wanted to reach into his mind now, but she didn't dare; she'd heard those being probed sometimes blacked out, and if he did that while he was driving like he was now—she clutched at the armrest as the car skidded around a sharp corner and squealed down a side road.

Rick punched a cassette into his stereo. Raucous music that even Maribeth's memories didn't help Liothel identify blared so loud she winced. The only label she could come up with that seemed to apply was "heavy metal." It fit. To Liothel it sounded like nothing so much as a troop of armored Warriors tumbling down the Mykia stairs.

There could be no conversation carried on above that horrendous din; Liothel was grateful for that much. Anyway, Maribeth's memories told her Rick wasn't much interested in conversation; there was really only one thing he wanted from a girl, and Liothel had already promised it to him.

They passed the last house of the city and the pavement gave way to snow-packed dirt. Ahead a copse of trees, left-overs from some long-vanished farmyard, bulked black against the star-filled sky. The Firebird's headlights swept over rows of dark trunks like prison bars as the car swung down in among the trees and stopped. Rick killed the headlights, though he left the engine running. He turned toward her, his eyes reflecting the green glow of the instrument panel. "Come here," he said, and pulled her to him.

Liothel's flesh crawled at his touch, and it was all she could do not to cringe when his lips crushed hers, but she forced herself to stay put, to let his hands rove where they would, while she closed her eyes and readied herself for the plunge into his mind....

She felt their seats go back, dimly felt Rick fumbling for the zipper of her coat and drawing it down, but then she made the leap and suddenly she was inside Rick's head, far deeper than she had gone into Adam's.

It was like plunging into a sewer. Vile images and feelings swirled around her like filthy currents of polluted sludge, tugging at her, threatening to pull her down. She could feel Rick's lust, throbbing at the core of his mind, and in shock she pulled herself free, both mentally and physically.

Rick stared at her, licking his lips, eyes bright. "You're not backing out on me again!" he growled.

Liothel blinked and swallowed rapidly. Her heart pounded frantically, as though trying to burst from her chest. "No..." she whispered. "No...of course not." But she couldn't bring herself to move closer, and so he seized her and yanked her hard against him, and his mouth, tasting sourly of stale cigarettes, enveloped hers once more.

He had slipped her coat off her sometime while she had been oblivious; now he was reaching inside her sweater, and she knew she was running out of time. With a prayer to the Creator, she closed her eyes and made the plunge once more.

This time she was prepared for the squalor, though still she shrank from that burning physical desire that seemed to drive everything else. Grimly she focused her mind, seeking that one thing she had to know—what Christine and the Ice Devils had planned.

Gradually it came to her, swimming up out of the murk like a snake surfacing in the slime of a swamp. It wasn't a distinct picture, or clear, unequivocal words, but suddenly she knew what the soulworm had put in place for its spawning, and when, and where: a fight, between the Ice Devils and a gang from Regina, Friday night, at the cemetery.

And then she was wrenched out of Rick's mind by pain, sharp and stinging. Her eyes jerked open and she found Rick glaring down at her, wild-eyed and breathing hard. "You're not even trying, you bitch!" he snarled. "What the hell are you playing at?"

She touched her bruised cheek, and for a moment felt terror. Escaping now that she had what she wanted might be impossible. She knew well enough from what she had felt in Rick's mind that he would rape her without a qualm if she resisted him. She hadn't really believed it before—but now she knew she had been naive. Maribeth might have been able to tell her—but only Maribeth's body was here now, and it was that body that was at risk.

But hard on the heels of that fear came anger, even rage, anger at Rick and sick anger at herself for sinking so low as to use Maribeth's body as bait. "Get away from me!" she screamed, and pushed him as hard as she could, up and back. His head cracked against the ceiling of the car and

181

he swore, then grabbed for her as she scrabbled for the door handle. She kicked blindly at him and he doubled over with a groan. The door finally opened and she tumbled out into the snow, then scrambled to her feet as Rick lurched out after her, getting one hand on her sweater. She jerked free, the sweater pulling half-down one arm, and ran into the dark, leaving her coat behind.

She expected him to come after her, but her kick seemed to have taken the fight out him, and she understood why when she saw him fall into the snow, curled into a ball, gasping for breath. Finally he heaved himself upright and clung to the car door, glaring around into the night. "Your turn is coming, bitch!" he screamed. "I owe you twice over now. You're mine! I don't care what Christine says, you're mine!"

Liothel crouched, shivering, until at last he finished swearing, got in his car and drove off in a cloud of snow and exhaust. She listened to the engine noise fading away, then, her arms wrapped around herself, began the walk back.

It was longer than she remembered, and much colder than the first time she had walked back after an evening with Rick, and by the time she reached the edge of town she knew she couldn't make it all the way home.

There were still lights on in the first house she came to; she made her way down the neatly shovelled walk and rang the doorbell. After a long pause the door opened a crack, revealing a weatherbeaten and suspicious bearded face. "Please," Liothel said between chattering teeth, "may I use your phone?"

The door closed and for a moment she despaired; but then she heard the sound of a chain being drawn back and soon, after a flurry of exclamations and introductions, she was sitting in a warm kitchen, a kettle filled with water just beginning to whistle, and the matronly silver-haired lady who shared the house with her retired-farmer husband laying a dozen different varieties of cookies on a plate. "I'd really better make that phone call, Mrs. Wanner," Liothel said.

"Of course, dear. Ed! Ed, bring the phone over here!"

Her husband, who hadn't said a word since letting Liothel in, set the phone on the table beside her. Liothel picked up the receiver and started to dial Maribeth's parents; then stopped. She didn't know what they'd do after this latest escapade, but she did know it was going to become almost impossible to see Adam alone, and she had to see him—had to tell him what she had learned, and what he had to do if they were going to defeat the soulworm.

So she aborted her call and started over, this time dialling Adam's number. A man answered sleepily after four rings. "Hello?"

"May I speak to Adam?"

"Do you know what time it is, young lady?" said the man, sounding a little more awake and on the verge of becoming angry.

"Yes, sir. But it's very important."

"Oh, for—just a minute." She heard vague noises, a woman's voice, then a shout, "Adam! Telephone! Take it downstairs—and be quiet about it. It's after midnight."

Liothel heard one phone being answered and another hung up, then Adam said, around a yawn, "Hello?"

"Adam, it's me—Liothel."

"Who? Oh—Maribeth."

Liothel didn't argue. "I need you to come pick me up."

"Pick you up? Where? What's happened?" He suddenly sounded much more alert.

She gave him the address. "I need a ride home."

"But why...?"

"I'll tell you later. Will you come?"

"My parents won't like it much—but, yeah, I'll come."

"Thanks. How quick can you be here?"

"Quick as I can get dressed and get the car rolling. Quicker if we both hang up now."

Liothel laughed, feeling a little hysterical with relief. "Okay," she said, and put the phone down; but she couldn't seem to stop laughing, and after a moment she realized the laughter had turned into tears. *Stop it!* she told herself in horror. *Nothing happened. You got away. You're not hurt—Maribeth's not hurt. And you found out what you had to know. Why are you crying?*

But she couldn't stop herself. She felt—unclean, as dirty as Kalia had been when she came to Mykia. She thought she could still feel Rick's hands on her borrowed body, the sour taste of his mouth, and in the back of her mind burned all too clearly the memory of his lust.

Mrs. Wanner put her arm around her. "There, there, child," she murmured. "Whatever happened, it's all over. It was a boy, wasn't it?"

"How—how did you know?" Liothel gulped out.

"It always is, lass, it always is." Mrs. Wanner glared at her husband, who was pushing tobacco into an ancient pipe with his calloused thumb. He ignored her. "Now, drink your hot chocolate and eat a cookie or two. You'll feel better."

"I doubt it," Liothel said, but she drank the chocolate anyway and stopped the trembling of her jaw with an Oreo, and to her surprise, she did feel better—shaky, and weak, and worn out, but no longer on the constant verge of tears.

Adam arrived fifteen minutes later. Mrs. Wanner glared at him when he stepped inside, stamping the snow from his running shoes, but Liothel smiled at her. "Different boy, Mrs. Wanner," she said. "Thank you for everything. I really appreciate it."

"My pleasure, dear. I hope everything works out for you."

"Thank you. Good-bye, Mr. Wanner!" The old man, puffing on his pipe, didn't say anything, but nodded his head a fraction of an inch. He and his wife both watched from the porch as Liothel followed Adam out to the Mustang.

They didn't talk until they were safely inside; then Adam, as he pulled away from the curb, said, "So give. What are you doing here, where's your coat, and what happened to your sweater?"

Liothel told him, leaving nothing out. Halfway through the story Adam swerved abruptly to the edge of the road and parked there. He listened to the rest of the tale staring straight ahead, and even in the dim light of the instruments Liothel could tell his hands were clenched hard on the steering wheel. "I'll kill him," he said when she finished. "So help me—"

"I hurt him worse than he hurt me," Liothel said.

"You were lucky. That pig would have—"

"I know what he would have done."

"Yeah?" Adam turned on her, suddenly raging. "So what right did you have? What right did you have to use Maribeth's body that way? Nothing would have happened to you—you can always just fly back to Never-Never Land, can't you? This is all some kind of mind game for you, isn't it? Like a big-scale Dungeons and Dragons?" He was shouting now. "Who invited you here? You come barging in, and suddenly Maribeth's gone, only she isn't gone, I can see her right in front of me, but she says she's someone else—dammit, whoever you are, why don't you just go home where you came from and leave us alone!"

Liothel swallowed. "Adam, I—"

"Forget it! I don't want to hear it!" He started the engine and roared back onto the road.

Liothel looked away, blinking back tears. She'd been stupid, hoping he might feel anything for her—he'd fallen in love with Maribeth, not her. She was just someone who had come between them. He didn't even want her around. They only had two days before the soulworm spawned, and now the only person besides herself who knew the danger, the only one who could help, wouldn't—couldn't—

I've failed, she thought miserably. *I've failed, and the soulworm has won. This world will fall to it, and it will be my fault. Even with two talents, I can't do the job. All I can do is mess up—mess up the plan to send Jara here, mess up Maribeth's life, mess up Adam's. I've got no business here—Adam's right, I should just go back where I came from.*

But I can't even do that.

The Mustang slowed, stopped. Liothel looked up and saw they were parked across the street from Maribeth's house. She fumbled for the door handle, not looking at Adam; but he reached out and touched her arm, and she froze.

"Liothel—I—I'm sorry," he said softly. "I was just—when I saw you in that house, with your face scratched up and bruised and your sweater torn, all I could think about was Maribeth. I wasn't really thinking of you—I know you were hurt too. Maribeth wasn't even there, not really." His face hardened. "But I'd still like to kill Trudgeon."

"If we don't stop Christine," Liothel said, unlooked-for hope suddenly filling her, "he'll be worse than dead. He'll be possessed. And all the things inside his head that make him like this—" she gestured at herself— "will be ten times worse."

"So what do we do?"

Liothel met his eyes. "You'll still help me? Even after—"

186

"Of course I will." His voice was gruff. "Just tell me what to do."

You don't stand a chance, the voice of doubt said again. *It's foolishness...*

She ignored it. "Thank you," she said. "Here's what we need..."

24

Mr. Gayle Puts His Foot Down

Adam sat in silence after Liothel finished talking. "It won't be easy," he said finally. "Getting her into the ring—setting the fire—and what are the Ice Devils going to be doing in the meantime?"

"They should be too busy fighting those Regina bikers."

"You'd better be right about this."

"I am."

He took a deep breath. "All right. I said I'll help you, and I will. I just hope you can do your part."

"There's nothing the thing inside Christine would like better than to get rid of me," Liothel said quietly. "It's already tried. I'm the perfect bait for this trap."

"Sometimes the bait gets eaten, even if the trap works."

"You don't have to tell me that." She covered Adam's hand on the steering wheel with her own. "I hope, when this is over, you and Maribeth..."

"Yeah." Adam looked at her for a moment, then unexpectedly leaned over and kissed her once on the lips. "For luck." He nodded at the house. "You'd better get going."

Liothel, stunned, sat frozen for a moment, then said, "Uh—yes," and opened the door as Adam started the Mustang. As he drove away she saw the front door of the house open, and Maribeth's father silhouetted against the hall light. She licked her lips (was it her imagination, or were they sweet from Adam's kiss?) then walked slowly across the road.

Mr. Gayle said nothing; as she reached the steps he stood aside and motioned her through the door. Head down, knowing miserably there was no explanation she could give that Maribeth's parents would understand or believe, Liothel walked into the hallway. Maribeth's mother stood in the doorway to the living room, her face pale and her eyes red. Liothel could tell at once she had been crying, and it hurt like a knife in her heart. "Mom...?"

The door slammed behind her. "Get in the living room," Maribeth's father said, anger simmering in his voice. "Now."

"Dad—"

"Now!" The anger boiled over.

Liothel scurried past Maribeth's mother, whose eyes widened as she took in Liothel's torn and dirty clothes. "What happened to you?"

"We'll get to that," Maribeth's father snapped, coming into the room after them. This time, none of them sat down. "First things first. Just what do you think you're doing, running out again after you were told to stay at home? Have you decided not to be a part of this family anymore? Because I swear, I'm about ready to throw you out of this house. I won't have you defying us like this! If you can't live by our rules, you don't belong here."

Liothel said nothing; only stood and looked at the floor, wishing she was somewhere else. She would rather have faced the soulworm alone than Maribeth's parents at that moment.

"You look at me when I'm talking to you!" Maribeth's father shouted. Reluctantly, Liothel did so. "What have you got to say for yourself?"

Liothel remained mute.

"Answer me!"

"John, maybe—" Maribeth's mother began.

"Don't John, maybe, me! I want to know if Maribeth is planning to move out or if she's going to start obeying us." He glared at Liothel. "Well?"

"I'm not moving out," Liothel said. "Dad, please don't—"

"Then you're going to start obeying us?"

Liothel's throat closed; she knew in two days' time she would have to sneak out again, and she couldn't bring herself to lie, not again. Instead she said nothing.

"I see," Mr. Gayle said, his voice suddenly dull. He sat down on the couch. "Maribeth, what's happened to you?"

Liothel's heart ached. "It's just—it's not your fault, Daddy, it's—this is just a bad time for me. I promise, things will change." One way or another.

"We're worried about you," Maribeth's mother said softly. "You break the rules, you disappear without a word—we thought you might have run away. We were going to call the police—"

"I wouldn't run away!"

"The Maribeth we used to know wouldn't," said Maribeth's father. "But you—you're like a different person. I don't understand you any more." He sounded more sad than angry now. "You've changed." He looked up at her, and for the first time it seemed to register on him what she looked like. "What happened to you?" He stood up suddenly, face flushing. "That Adam—"

"It wasn't him," Liothel said hurriedly. "He just gave me a ride home."

"From where?"

190

"I—" Again her throat closed. She couldn't tell Maribeth's parents she had used their daughter's body to find out what she needed to know—or that she would soon be using their daughter's body as bait in a deadly trap. "I'd rather not talk about it."

"Maribeth, please—"

Liothel shook her head. "I—I just can't tell you. Please try to understand."

Maribeth's father shook his head. "We're trying, Maribeth. But you're not making it easy."

"I'm sorry."

"It takes more than just saying it."

Silence. Liothel stirred uncomfortably. Finally Maribeth's mother said, with forced cheerfulness, "Maribeth, your father and I think it would be a good idea if we all went away somewhere together, someplace away from Christine and Adam...maybe drive out to the lake. It's quiet out there, we can talk."

Liothel forced a smile. "It sounds great, Mom."

"Good," Mr. Gayle said flatly. "We're going this weekend. And when we come back we're going to have this thing straightened out."

Liothel's heart leaped. "But Dad, I can't, not this weekend."

"Why not?"

Because I'm going to risk your daughter's life and my own and Adam's to try to save your world from destruction? Liothel didn't think that would go over too well. "I—I have a date. With Adam." She knew the minute it was out of her mouth it was the wrong thing to say.

"With Adam? The same Adam we told you we don't want you to see? The same Adam that brought you home tonight looking like that?"

"I told you, he didn't—"

"Yes, you told me. Now I'm telling you—you're not seeing Adam. Not this weekend, not next weekend, not ever. Understand? And you're coming to the lake with us. Right after school is out on Friday. Do I make myself clear?"

Liothel opened her mouth to argue; closed it again, then said helplessly, "Yes."

"Good. Now go to bed."

Mutely, Liothel passed between her parents, into the hall and up the stairs. At the top sat Sean, in pajamas, hugging his legs to his chest. He looked at her wide-eyed as she approached. "Wow, Maribeth. You really got yourself in deep this time."

Liothel leaned wearily against the railing. "I know."

Sean stood up. "If—you know, if there's anything I can do to help—"

She smiled a little. "Thanks."

"Well—good night."

"Good night."

With a last backward glance, he disappeared down the hall to his room, and Liothel made her way into Maribeth's, where she lay on the bed without turning on the light and stared up at the faint pattern on the ceiling made by a streetlight shining through the frosted window. Maribeth's parents planned to drag her off to the lake precisely when her final confrontation with Christine would be brewing. That meant when they came looking for her after school on Friday, she couldn't be there.

And beyond a doubt, that meant they would think she had run away.

She was tearing apart Maribeth's family, the closest thing to a family she had ever had, and there wasn't a thing she could do about it.

Jara, why didn't you ever teach us anything about this! she cried silently; but if, across the mystical barrier that separated her from her own world, the Warders heard her cry, they could not or would not reply.

At least Adam was still on her side, she thought; and though she knew Maribeth was the one he loved, still she recalled the sweetness of his mouth on hers and, vows or no vows, let it warm her into sleep.

Breakfast was not a happy meal. The usual morning chatter was replaced by a kind of strained politeness, as though they had all suddenly become strangers. Maribeth's father left earlier than usual, and so did Liothel. Even Sean was on his way to school five minutes before his usual departure time.

As Liothel entered the school building, she heard the sound of the Ice Devils' cars arriving. She didn't look back.

But only an hour later she saw the two gang members she most dreaded seeing together: Christine and Rick. Liothel stood half-hidden behind the trophy case and watched them at the far end of the hallway, by the door to the library. Rick was backed against the wall and Christine stood over him, only inches away, her mouth working furiously, though Liothel couldn't hear a word. Silently she fretted. What if Christine—the soulworm—realized Liothel had discovered when the spawning was to occur? What would she/it do?

Abruptly Christine stepped back, and Rick scurried away like a scolded puppy. And then Christine's eyes swung toward Liothel, and even at that distance they seemed to glint red. Slowly Liothel emerged from behind the trophy case. For a long moment the two girls stared at each other across the tiled floor, oblivious to the students and teachers who swirled and eddied around them. Maribeth's memories provided Liothel with the image of two gunfighters facing each other on a dusty Western street; there could be no confrontation here and now, but they both knew it was coming—and coming soon.

But then Christine did something that frightened Liothel as much as the moment on that dark plain of the imagination when the dragon had loomed above her: she smiled, showing her teeth, bone-white beneath the fluorescent lights. And then she spun and strode away, vanishing a moment later around the corner at the end of the hall.

Liothel stayed where she was, staring blankly at the place where Christine had been, while the hallways emptied around her and the final bell rang. Her mind raced. That smile—what did Christine know? And what would she do about it? If she and Adam had lost the element of surprise...

She had to talk to him, warn him. She hurried on to the library, her original destination, hoping he might be there, at least counting on seeing him later in the day, but though she craned her head at every break, searched every corridor in the course of the morning, not once did she glimpse his lanky form. Over lunch she found out why. "He's supposedly sick," Crystal confided, "but I saw his Mustang heading out of town this morning."

Liothel's heart lurched. "Out of town?" Had he run out on her after all?

"Toward Regina." Crystal gave her a concerned look. "Hey, are you all right? You look funny!"

"I'm—fine."

"Sure you are. I told you not to eat the green beans."

Liothel told herself not to worry, that Adam wouldn't leave her on her own. But Crystal's news made the winter air feel even colder as she walked home from school that afternoon.

It was both a relief and a worry when, about nine o'clock that night, the phone rang. Liothel was in the living room, watching with bemusement a television program Sean seemed to find hilarious but she, even with Maribeth's memories to draw on, could make no sense of at all. She heard Maribeth's mother answer the phone. "Hello?...Yes, she's here. Who is this, please?...Adam?"

Liothel stiffened, but before she could get up Maribeth's father stormed out of the room. "You listen to me, Adam," she heard him say, "and listen good, because I'm not going to repeat it. Our daughter is not to see you again, is that clear? And that means I don't want you calling her, talking to her, or so much as saying hello to her on the way to school. You understand me?...Good. And good-bye!"

The receiver crashed down, and Sean shot Liothel a wide-eyed look. She turned back to the television, but saw nothing. Adam hadn't left her—but why was he calling? Had something gone wrong? Had he learned something she had to know?

Maribeth's father had made it impossible for her to find out, or to tell Adam about her own worrisome fears. Tomorrow she would have to face Christine and the soulworm, and she would have to do so knowing that the creature might be forewarned—and without knowing whether her sole ally was in fact prepared to do what would have to be done if the creature were to be stopped.

She found it very hard to concentrate on the inane antics of the tiny figures on the glowing screen.

25

The Cemetery

The temperature soared overnight, and by early morning had almost reached freezing. "Looks like we're going to lose some snow," Maribeth's father said at breakfast, his first words all morning. "At least we'll have good weather for the drive to the lake tonight. Pack what you need before you leave this morning, Maribeth, and we'll pick you up right after school."

Liothel nodded, and though she knew she was not going to the lake, she nevertheless went upstairs after breakfast and put a few clothes into a duffel bag, which she set by the front door on her way out. Maribeth's father had already left for work, but her mother waved a tentative good-bye from the kitchen door.

"Hey, Maribeth, wait up!" she heard behind her as she reached the end of the front walk, and she turned to see Sean running after her, coat unbuttoned and hair uncombed. "Let me walk with you."

Liothel looked at him curiously. "Your school's in the other direction."

"Yeah, well, I'm early anyway."

Liothel stared at him, then laughed and shrugged. "All right."

They traversed the first block without speaking, then Sean said, "You're planning to skip out on this trip to the lake, aren't you?"

Liothel almost stumbled in surprise. "What makes you say that?"

Sean snorted. "Give me a break. I've been figuring out what you're going to do before you do it for years. Face it, big sister, I can read you like a book."

Apparently even though I'm not his sister, Liothel thought. *He should be a Sentinel.* After they had walked in silence for moment, she said, "Do you think Mom and Dad know?"

"Naw. They're just worried their pwecious wittle girl is going bad on them." He shot her a look. "You're not, are you? I mean, you're not into drugs or—or—well, you know."

Liothel smiled slightly. "No, I'm not into drugs or 'you know.'"

Sean relaxed a little. "Well, that's a relief. I'd hate to be the only kid in my class with a sister in reform school." He stopped, and Liothel stopped with him. "Look, I'd better get going. I just wanted to know—you know, if you were in trouble. You're—well, you know, you're not bad—for a big sister." His face turned bright red.

Liothel's smile broadened. "Thanks. And you're not bad either—for a little brother."

"I don't suppose you'll change your mind about going to the lake...no, I didn't think so." Sean sighed. "Well, when the yelling starts, try to keep it down, will you? You guys make it hard to sleep." With a wave he turned and trotted back the way they had come.

Liothel walked on, her mood brightened by the unexpected support from her little brother....

Not your little brother, the cruel voice that had surfaced two nights before snapped. *Maribeth's little brother. You think he'd be on your side if he knew who and what you really are? He's worried his sister is involved in something dangerous—he doesn't know the half of it. And all the danger is because of you!*

By the time Liothel reached school, her spirits had fallen twice as low as they had been before.

Classes passed in a blur; Liothel knew Maribeth would be in serious academic trouble when—and if—she returned, but she had more pressing matters to worry about. She'd already decided to avoid Maribeth's parents by the simple expedient of slipping out of the school through a different door than the one she usually used. Then she'd head for what she already thought of as "the spawning ground"—the cemetery. She had no doubt the soulworm had chosen the location for its own perverse amusement. Christine's memories must contain the same horror-movie images as Maribeth's. A series of films containing the strange phrase "Living Dead" seemed to predominate...

Adam had promised to skip out of his last two classes of the day in order to prepare things there. By the time she arrived, he would either have done so, or—

—or else he wouldn't show. The memory of the phone call the night before haunted her.

Christine and the Ice Devils were nowhere to be seen that day, and Liothel thought she was probably the only one who missed them. Even when she wasn't thinking about it consciously, subconsciously her mind kept churning out horrifying new scenarios of what might happen if Christine knew her plans were no longer secret—more horrifying than Maribeth's gory film memories. *What if they went to the spawning ground early, and caught Adam at his preparations? What if they changed the location? What if—what if—what if?*

There was nothing she could do about it. For better or worse (*for worse*, said that nagging voice) her plans were laid.

The final bell rang. Liothel stood up from her desk in the English Lit. room and somehow navigated the halls to Maribeth's locker, without quite remembering how she had done it.

"...do tonight?" someone asked her.

For a moment she looked blankly at Crystal, not recognizing her; then said, "I'm sorry, what—?"

Crystal exchanged a significant look with Ellen. "I told you. She's in love."

"With Adam," said Ellen, fluttering her eyelashes. "Maribeth, we know he drives a Mustang—does that mean he's a real stud?"

Liothel stared at them both. The banter that Maribeth's memories had normally supplied her with so easily, that had made her impersonation of the other girl work, escaped her. "Excuse me," she said finally. "I've got to go—"

She brushed past Maribeth's friends, barely hearing Crystal call after her, "Maribeth, wait, we're sorry..."

It was just after four, she noted as she passed under the clock at the end of the hall. It would be fully dark by six, but Christine's special "party" wasn't scheduled to begin until at least eleven. Liothel had a feeling the next seven hours would be the longest she had ever endured.

A moment later she was out of the building. It took her only a second to realize her mistake, but by then it was too late; preoccupied, she had come out the way Maribeth usually did, and right there in front of her was her father's blue Chrysler—and Maribeth's parents.

Her shock wasted the only instant in which she could have run; Maribeth's father was already rounding the front of the car to meet her. "I was beginning to wonder if you would show up." His voice was too harsh to be entirely joking. "We've put your bag in the car; get in."

His hand gripped her arm; helplessly she followed him to the car and climbed into the back seat. Her father got into the driver's seat. For a moment panic gripped Liothel; then she found her voice. "Dad," she said, as he started the car, "could you stop at the gas station before we pick up Sean? I need to use the washroom."

"Why didn't you—oh, never mind. All right. I can top off the tank."

Liothel sat back and bit her lower lip until the car halted at the pumps of the PetroCan station across the street from the 7-11. "I'll just be a minute," she said, and went around the corner, following the sign marked "Restrooms," while behind her Mr. Gayle opened the flap of the gas tank.

She reached the green-painted door with the crooked metal image of a figure in a dress on it—and kept going, breaking into a run. Behind the gas station was the alley that led to the Colosseum, and she ducked down it. As she took one final look back, she thought she saw someone waving at her from the 7-11 parking lot, and she ran even faster. If whoever-it-was shouted to her parents...

Past the Colosseum she plunged at random off the road into someone's front yard, ploughed through melting snowdrifts to the back yard, ran across another alley, dashed through someone else's yard, and then took to the street beyond that.

Several more streets, two alleys and one barking dog later, she leaned against the wall of a dilapidated garage and took deep breaths. She hated to think of Maribeth's parents believing their daughter had run away, but...

She stiffened at the sound of a siren. Had they called the police?

The siren kept going, and she relaxed—a little. No, of course not. The police wouldn't do anything until she'd been missing twenty-four hours—at least, that's what Maribeth had believed. And in twenty-four hours, one way or another, everything would be settled.

Her breathing back to normal, she trudged on down the alley, splashing through puddles. There was very little wind and the sky was cloudless; it might have been spring, instead of late January. *A good night for a fire*, she thought, and hurried on.

When she reached the downtown she ducked into the Weyburn Square mall to warm up and to kill time. She still had hours to wait. She had a little money with her and used it to buy a sandwich and hot chocolate; she took her time eating and drinking, her eyes flicking constantly from the restaurant's front entrance to the back one that led out into the parking lot, expecting at any moment to see her father looking for her...but he never appeared.

She left the mall as the sun was setting, and followed Government Road across the river and up and over the northern shoulder of the hill on which Mykia stood in her world. Off to her left she could see the lights of the hospital where Maribeth had awakened, with Liothel tucked away inside, an unwanted passenger. But her destination lay straight ahead: the city cemetery.

The spawning ground.

A vehicle roared past her, and she flinched; but it was a pick-up, not a Firebird. Nonetheless, she descended into the still-snow-filled ditch to get away from the direct glare of the headlights coming and going. The Ice Devils might arrive at any minute to prepare for their Regina "guests," and even if they didn't, Maribeth's father was probably out on the roads, looking for his daughter.

The cemetery gate loomed ahead, silhouetted against the last, fading light of the winter sky. That same light gave the headstones beyond it a ghostly white glow. The air was absolutely still and breathless—and rapidly growing colder.

Liothel hunched her coat closer around her and, arms folded, crept up to the gate. It was chained shut, but there was plenty of room between the gate bars for someone on foot to slip through.

Liothel's feet crunched on the white gravel that covered the road beyond the gate. She stopped and looked around—and saw movement off to her left, beside the maintenance equipment shed. Her heart speeded suddenly. *Adam, or...?*

She dared not cry out. Instead she crept closer to the shed, slipping around headstones, trying not to walk on the graves themselves through some obscure impulse that had to arise from Maribeth, since she had no fear of the dead in her own world.

She stopped suddenly and listened. The evening's stillness had given way to a rising wind that whispered over the snow, masking lesser sounds. But she thought she had heard a sound like—

She barely choked off a scream as a dark shape rose from behind a headstone to her right, and said in a deep voice, "Liothel?"

"Adam?" she breathed, relief flooding her.

"Yeah." He came over to her. "I thought you might be—"

"One of the Ice Devils?"

"Or a biker." He motioned toward the shed. "I've set everything up over there—it was the only bit of cleared ground I could find, and I didn't think it would work in the snow."

"You're probably right. I hadn't thought about it." Liothel trudged over to the maintenance shack, Adam trailing. A sharp, oily scent filled her nostrils. "You didn't have any trouble finding the stuff?"

"No. I went up to Regina for it yesterday."

"Couldn't you have bought it here?"

"I could have, but the Ice Devils would have been more likely to find out about it." She sensed him looking at her in the dark. "Why?"

"Oh...nothing."

"You thought I'd run out on you, didn't you?" he said quietly.

She didn't reply.

He took her arms and turned her to look at him, though his face was only an indistinct pale patch. "Trust me. I am on your side. I believe you. And I won't desert you, whatever happens."

"Me—or Maribeth?" The words slipped out before Liothel realized what they implied.

Adam stiffened, then let go of her arms. "It's a little hard for me to make that distinction, OK?" He turned away. "Let me show you what I've done. I've got a flashlight here somewhere..."

"Wait!" Liothel grabbed his wrist. "Adam, I'm sorry! I didn't really believe you'd left me—or Maribeth. But I was frightened." She told him what had passed between her and Christine outside the library.

He gave a low whistle when she finished. "What will we do if she knows we're here?" He paused. "More to the point, what will she do?"

"There's only one thing we can do," Liothel said miserably. "We have to try to carry out our plan."

"But—"

"We have to try!" It burst out of Liothel in an anguished cry. "Adam, I don't know if I could defeat that soulworm even back home, with the whole Wardfast to help. I've never had to face one alone—I was only an Acolyte in Mykia. But here—I'm all alone, the only one who can stop it. All I can do is try, even if I don't think I can win—and to tell you the truth, Adam, I don't!" Her voice fell off to a whisper. "I don't."

Adam pulled her to him and put his arms around her. For a moment she stiffened, but the warmth of his body melted her resistance, and his strong arms kept her there. "You're wrong about one thing," he said huskily. "You're not alone."

Tears ran icy rivulets down her cheeks, until she pressed her face against his chest; and for once, she didn't think about her vows, or about whether Adam's attraction was to her or to Maribeth.

He led her to the toolshed, and with their backs to it, still clinging to each other, they settled down to wait.

26

The Soulworm Strikes

Warm in Adam's arms, listening to the slow rhythm of his heartbeat, Liothel let her mind drift, thinking of nothing in particular. Their dice were cast, their wager made; they could only await the outcome. Slowly, without even being aware of it, she slipped over the edge into sleep...

...and woke, shivering. Adam slept beside her, his arms having slipped away from her, his head lolling forward on his chest. She looked around, confused. What time was it? Where were the Ice Devils? Where were the Regina bikers? Where was the soulworm?

"Adam! Adam, wake up!" Liothel shook him. "Adam!"

He groaned and lifted his head, blinking at her. "Wha—" She could almost see realization rushing into him. "What's going on? Are they here?"

"No! But they should be. Can you read your watch?"

He lifted his wrist and pressed something. A faint light illuminated tiny numbers. "It's after midnight. Way after."

Liothel scrambled to her feet and listened. No powerful motors rumbled through the night; nothing moved on the highway outside the cemetery gates. "Creator's blood," she whispered. "We've lost."

"What?" Adam also struggled up. "Why?"

"Don't you see?" Liothel turned toward him, despair squeezing her heart with fingers of ice. "The Ice Devils didn't come. They called it off. Christine—the soulworm—knows we're here."

"Then it won't be spawning? But doesn't that mean we've won?"

"No, you don't understand! It will still spawn—but not here. It will create the violence it needs somewhere else, somewhere we're—uh!"

"Liothel? Liothel! What's wrong?"

Liothel hardly heard him; barely felt his hands holding her up. Ringing in her head was a call of savage power, a scream of joy and defiance that could only have come from one source—the soulworm. Somewhere out in the city it had begun the process of spawning. Somewhere, violence was being brewed.

And suddenly Liothel knew where, before she could even use her Gift to locate it, the knowledge rising sure and terrifying from the intuition in the heart she shared with Maribeth. "Home!" she screamed.

"Liothel?"

Liothel tore free of Adam's hands, stumbled toward the gate. "She's attacking my—Maribeth's—our home!"

Adam ran after her, caught her arms, though she writhed like a snake. "Liothel, wait! Settle down! Not that way—this way."

"But—"

"Do you plan to run the whole way? My car's parked by the back gate!"

Liothel quit struggling and ran after him down the white-gravelled paths of the cemetery, stones crunching beneath their feet, their breath puffing out in great clouds of steam in the cold air, lit by the moon high above and the brilliant Saskatchewan stars. Adam reached the gate first and scrambled up and over the bars; by the time Liothel squeezed between them the Mustang's big motor throbbed with impatient power, and the moment she was inside Adam accelerated away, spraying the cemetery wall with gravel as he roared toward the highway.

Liothel stared blindly out the windshield at the swath of pavement illuminated by the headlights. Adam scarcely slowed as they swept under the yellow-orange glare of the Government Road streetlights, weaving around the few other cars on the street; even so, a police car raced past them, lights flashing, ignoring the Mustang that any other time would have been prime prey. As they neared the 7-11 the police car skidded left around the corner, running a red light. In the absence of oncoming traffic, Adam followed suit. Ahead a red glow suffused the sky. The police car turned toward it, Adam followed—and Liothel's worst fears were realized.

Flames licked the roof of the Gayles' house and roared from the upstairs windows. Half a dozen helmeted men in heavy canvas coats and rubber boots poured water on the fire from three hoses. Ice sheathed the walls, the lower windows, the porch, but Liothel could tell it was already too late; the house was lost, and everything inside it.

Everything—

Before the Mustang was completely stopped Liothel threw open the door and jumped out, tripping and sprawling across the pavement but scrambling up and running down the sidewalk, knees and hands scraped and bloody. A burly policeman grabbed her as she tried to pass the barricades that surrounded the lawn. "Wait a minute, miss, you can't—"

"That's my house!" she screamed at him. "Where are my parents? Where's my little brother?"

"You're Maribeth Gayle?" The policeman didn't let go of her, but turned and called, "Sergeant! The Gayles' girl just turned up!"

A smaller man in a rumpled uniform rounded one of the police cars and came toward them, rubbing his chin with one hand. Liothel's knees went weak with relief as, over his shoulder, she saw Maribeth's parents sitting in the back seat of the car in their night clothes, blankets clutched around their shoulders, Miser shivering on their laps.

"So you're the prodigal daughter?" said the sergeant. He nodded toward the house. "Not much of a homecoming."

"How are my parents? And Sean?"

"Your parents are as well as can be expected." The sergeant's gaze never left her face. "Under the circumstances."

Liothel closed her eyes and offered a silent prayer of thanks to the Creator; then frowned, filled with sudden foreboding. "What about Sean?"

"As far as we know, he's fine, too." The sergeant fished in his pocket for a package of cigarettes.

"What do you mean, as far as you know? Isn't he with my parents?"

"No." The sergeant lit his cigarette with a match taken from a paper book.

"Then where—?" Understanding hit Liothel like a physical blow, and she gasped with the pain. "Christine has him!"

"Very interesting you should think so." Smoke wreathed the sergeant's words. "Considering I didn't tell you anything about anyone named Christine."

"She did this, didn't she?" Liothel looked at the burning house, as a window exploded outward in a shower of red-glittering glass. "She and her Ice Devils." She glanced back at Maribeth's parents, holding on to each other in the car, and something like a fire kindled inside her, too.

"You seem to know an awful lot about it, Miss Gayle." The sergeant's voice was sharp, now. "Would you mind telling me how?"

Liothel opened her mouth—then closed it again. "I heard rumors they were going to do something—big," she said finally. "But I didn't think they'd go this far...."

"Neither did we—even though we've been keeping an eye on them. We thought they were planning some sort of free-for-all with a Regina motorcycle gang, to establish their reputation. But this—" He gestured at the house. "They didn't even try to hide who was doing it. They came roaring up in those big cars of theirs, carrying guns—Lord knows where they got those—kicked in the front door, grabbed your little brother right out of bed, threw your parents out onto the lawn and torched the place—all in less than ten minutes. The whole neighborhood saw them leaving. We were here three minutes later—but they were gone." He dropped the cigarette onto the sidewalk and ground it into the concrete with his heavy black shoe. "I just don't understand what they hope to accomplish. The RCMP are sending a SWAT team down from Regina. They don't stand a chance." He glanced back at the police car. "I think you're parents would like to see you."

Liothel took half a step forward—and stopped. No. She had just called them her parents, had thought of them as her parents, had felt their pain as if they were her own—but they weren't. They were Maribeth's, and all Liothel had brought them was ruin. She had destroyed their relationship with their daughter, and now she had destroyed their home, as surely as if she had set the fire herself. The best thing she could do for them was to leave them. Christine wouldn't bother them again—she had what she wanted. SWAT, the sergeant had said. Special Weapons and Tactics. Violence.

Maribeth's memories gave her all the images she needed to know that when that team moved in on the Ice Devils, the soulworm would find ample violence for it to complete the spawning it had already begun, to burst the bounds of Christine's mind and swarm into the unsuspecting world.

How dare it, she thought in cold fury, fury that for the first time was stronger than her uncertainty and fear. *How dare it ruin people's lives! How dare it put Sean in danger—worse, put him in a place where he, too, might fall under a soulworm's possession.*

She had no time to talk to Maribeth's parents; no time, if she were to find Christine and deal with the soulworm herself, before an "anonymous tip" reached the police and they brought their automatic weapons and tear gas to bear. And Maribeth's parents didn't really want to talk to her, anyway—they wanted to talk to their daughter, the daughter that still hid somewhere deep in her own brain.

Liothel couldn't give them back their daughter—not yet, anyway—but by the Creator, and with His help, she would give them back their son—and, though they didn't know it, their world.

The chimney of the house crashed through the roof, sending flames and sparks swirling skyward in wreaths of black smoke. "No, sergeant," Liothel said. "Tell them I'm fine, and I'll talk to them later—but not now. Not here."

The sergeant stared at her. "I'll tell them, young lady. But stick around, because I do want to talk to you—now. And here."

Liothel made no response. The sergeant strode toward the car, and Liothel at once turned and walked toward Adam, who had remained by the Mustang, watching the fire.

The policeman who had first stopped her called after her, but she ignored him. She nodded to Adam as she approached, and he scrambled into the driver's seat and fired

210

the engine. As Liothel opened her door she heard the policeman's heavy footfalls on the concrete; but before he reached her she was already inside and had locked the door behind her.

The Mustang's tires squealed as Adam U-turned and sped away, and Liothel, looking in the side mirror, saw the policeman shaking his head and walking back toward the sergeant's car.

"They may come after us," Adam said.

"I don't think so. I think the sergeant only wanted me around so he could try to get me back with my—Maribeth's parents."

"Why wouldn't you talk to them?"

"Because I don't have time. Turn right."

Adam complied, rounding onto First Avenue, heading north, toward the edge of town. "What do you mean, you don't have time? Where are we going?"

Liothel looked at him. "I hope you meant what you said about being my side," she said quietly. "Because we're going to go after Christine and the soulworm ourselves, now, before the police find them and the shooting starts."

"But—how? They could be anywhere."

"Don't worry." Liothel tapped her head. "I'll know where to look."

27

The Circle
Of Fire

Adam said nothing for a few minutes, while Liothel closed her eyes and concentrated on following that faint..."scent" seemed to be the only word for it, a scent like burning, like she had sensed from Kalia in the beginning. It had a definite location, somewhere ahead of them, growing slowly, slowly stronger. They were going in the right direction....

"This is crazy," Adam said abruptly. "Liothel, it's crazy. If you know where Christine and the Ice Devils are you should tell the police. What's to keep them from killing Sean—not to mention us!—if we just barge in on them by ourselves?"

"No police." Liothel kept her eyes closed. "That's what Christine is hoping for. She'll tell them herself where she and the Ice Devils are when she's ready. What better environment for the soulworm to spawn in than a shootout between the Devils and the police?"

"But Sean..."

"She won't kill Sean. He's her bait."

"And we're taking it!"

Liothel opened her eyes and looked at him. He drove mechanically, staring straight ahead, his jaw clenched and his hands tight on the wheel. "You don't have to come. You can let me off, and I'll walk if I have to. I have a duty—you don't."

"I said I'd stick by you, and I meant it," Adam growled. "I'm not backing out on you. But nobody said I had to like it."

"I don't like it much myself." Liothel's eyes suddenly widened. "Turn left!"

"Where?"

"Wherever you can—we're going past them!"

A grid road crossed the highway just ahead; Adam braked precipitously and fishtailed onto it, wheels throwing gravel and snow. He drove out among the dark fields, while Liothel closed her eyes again and concentrated. "We're getting close," she whispered. "Not far now...off to the right..."

"There's a lot of trees over there," Adam said. "Windbreaks—looks like an old farm."

"Then that's it. Stop the car!"

Adam pulled over and killed the engine. The whistling of the wind around the Mustang's sheetmetal filled the sudden silence. "Now what?"

"I'm hoping that the soulworm doesn't sense me the way I sense it. I don't think it can, so close to spawning; it will be working itself into a frenzy. All its concentration will be on what it's about to do. We should be able to sneak up on it."

"On it, maybe," Adam said. "But don't forget all those Ice Devils. With guns."

Liothel said nothing.

"And what about what you told me before? The Circle of Fire and all the rest of it? What good will it do you to face the soulworm if you don't have that ready? Your Circle of Fire is back in the cemetery."

"We'll have to improvise. You've still got a can of gasoline in the back, don't you? And matches?"

"Yes, but—"

Suddenly furious, Liothel turned on him. "You think I have all the answers?" she cried. "I don't! I don't know what I'm going to do. I told you back in the cemetery—I don't even think I have much of a chance. But I've got to at least try—or everything that's happened, all the trouble I've caused Maribeth, and her parents, and now Sean..." For a moment her throat closed, then she choked out, "Either help me or get out of my way!" Fumbling for the latch, she pushed open the door, scrambled out of the Mustang and dashed into the field.

"Liothel! Liothel, wait!" Adam ran after her, caught her by her arm and spun her around. "Liothel, I'm sorry!" He gripped her shoulders, his face pale in the moonlight, his eyes bright. "I was just—talking to hear myself talk." His voice dropped to a whisper. "I'm scared."

Liothel shivered. "Oh, Adam," she breathed. "So am I. So am I!"

Then Adam's arms were around her, holding her; and somehow their lips met, and this time Liothel did not pull away, or think about her vows or whether he cared for her or for Maribeth. Instead she drank in the comfort, the human contact, feeding on it like the soulworm fed on hatred. She needed every immaterial ounce of it to fuel her for what was to come.

At last their lips parted. Adam pulled her to him so tightly her ribs creaked, but she didn't mind. "Liothel...Maribeth..." he whispered. "If anything happens to you..."

Gently Liothel pushed free. "We'd better go. The police may already be on their way." She waited while he opened the Mustang's hatchback and took out a half-full five-gallon gasoline can; then, hand in hand, they continued across the stubbled field to the line of darker black that was the old farm's windbreak.

Dry branches creaked and snapped as they pushed their way through them, but the wind masked the noise so that Liothel had no fear of anyone up ahead hearing them. At last they emerged on the edge of the farmyard. The Ice Devils' Firebirds were drawn up around the old wooden house like wagons in a Western Maribeth had once seen. Lights flickered and bobbed from window to window; flashlights. Upstairs a single light burned steadily. Liothel's eyes were drawn to it like a moth to a candle flame. "Christine's up there," she whispered. "And probably, so is Sean."

"How do we get past the Ice Devils?"

Liothel studied the house. The trees surrounding it hadn't been pruned in at least thirty years. Several branches scraped the roof as the wind tossed them restlessly. "We go over them. Or I do."

Adam followed her gaze. "It might work," he said slowly. "What do you want me to do?"

"I need you to get the Ice Devils outside. Can you hotwire a car?"

"I think so."

She pointed at the Firebirds. "If you start one of those up once I'm outside the window—"

"—the Ice Devils will come running." Adam's face looked even paler than before. "Or start shooting. Liothel, are you sure...?"

"Don't ask." Seemingly of its own accord, her hand reached out and caressed his cheek. "I'm sorry I got you involved in all this."

He covered her hand with his own, then leaned forward and kissed her again. "You'd better get going." He pressed a book of matches into her hand, then turned and scrambled away into the darkness.

Liothel swallowed a lump in her throat and, on legs threatening to tremble, crept toward the house through the deep shadow of the windbreak. When at last she judged she was out of the line of sight of any of the windows, near where an old water tank stood up against the house on rickety wooden scaffolding, she dashed across the lawn. Back pressed flat against the peeling white paint of the wall, she gulped cold air.

The "smell" of burning was overpowering, almost choking. The soulworm's spawning awaited only the final trigger of violence. She wondered how near the RCMP SWAT team was.

She inched her way along the wall until she was opposite one of the trees whose branches touched the first-story roof. A moment later she swarmed up it, hands and knees gripping the rough bark. She rested for a few seconds in a crotch at the top of the main trunk, then eased out over the empty space between tree and house, keeping her eyes on that single lit upstairs window. The branch swayed in the wind as though trying to throw her off, but she hung on and dropped onto the slanting shingles just below her goal.

Now, she silently urged Adam. Now!

For a long moment she clung there in silence, beginning to fear he could not see her, wondering how long it would be before Christine looked out the window; but then an engine roared to life in the farmyard below and raced as though about to tear itself apart. Headlights speared the darkness and shouting erupted downstairs. Seizing the moment, Liothel scrambled up the icy slope of the roof, ready to leap through the window glass if she had to, hoping her coat would protect her—but she didn't have to.

Christine threw open the window and leaned out just before Liothel reached it.

Their eyes met, Christine's burning red with the naked power of the soulworm. She reached up to slam the window closed, but Liothel hurled herself up and through it, crashing into Christine, tumbling with her into a heap on the floor, Liothel on top. She scrambled to her feet and shot a glance around. Sean, wearing only torn and dirty pajama bottoms, shivered on the floor in the corner, his wide eyes staring at her over a filthy gag, his arms tied behind him with yellow nylon rope. She lunged toward him, but Christine seized her from behind and threw her against the wall with incredible strength. Half-stunned, she clung to the cracked plaster and looked back over her shoulder at the soulworm-possessed girl. "So you found me." Christine's voice echoed oddly in Liothel's head, half sound, half the inner voice of the soulworm. "I didn't think you could. But now that you have, just what do you expect to be able to do to stop me?"

"Maybe nothing," Liothel said, panting. "But I have to try."

"Why?" Christine took a step toward Liothel, fists clenched. "Why can't you just leave well enough alone? Your kind has almost driven the Ancient Race out of our own world. Isn't that enough for you? Why must you meddle in this world, too?"

"You would destroy this world. People have a right to live their lives without your interference!"

"This world is destroying itself already!" the soulworm spat through Christine. "Why shouldn't we make use of it? Don't we have a right to live? We didn't create your hate—you did that. You humans hate each other all the time. We could live off overwhelming love, too—but there isn't enough of that. There's lots of hate! Why blame us? Why hunt us down and destroy us?"

"We hate—but you cultivate that hate," Liothel cried. "If you cultivated love the way you cultivate hate, maybe there would be enough of it for you to live on. And then we wouldn't have to fight you."

"Cultivate love? Would you live on gruel when you could have meat?" Christine took another step toward her. "You can't stop me, Warder. Tonight I spawn! The police will be here within minutes. My followers will fight, and as the blood-lust rages, I will spawn, and my children will claim first my followers and then the police themselves..." She smiled, like a vicious dog showing its teeth. "But first I think I'll let Rick have you—"

Footsteps sounded outside the door. Christine's smile widened. "That could be him now. I think I'll watch—to whet my appetite—"

The door crashed inward and Liothel's heart leaped as Adam burst in, panting, clutching the can of gasoline. With a furious howl, Christine spun toward him, and at once Liothel dashed to Sean, yanked the loop of rope from his wrists, then thrust him out the window onto the roof. The room filled with the sharp smell of gasoline as Adam sloshed the liquid liberally along the walls. Christine's eyes widened, then she screamed, "Ice Devils! Help!" and bolted for the door, but Adam dropped the gasoline canister and grabbed her, holding her as she clawed and spat like a cat. Christine's strength, even boosted by the soulworm's berserker rage, was no match for his. Liothel finished dousing the walls, threw the canister out the window, took out the matchbook Adam had given her, and touched flame to the gasoline-soaked wood.

Fire erupted around the room and Christine stiffened and shrieked horribly. The heat struck Liothel like a blow; her body erupted into sweat as she staggered back to the center of the room. Adam's face glistened with perspiration as he

218

released Christine, who no longer struggled, but stood, swaying. "The Circle of Fire..." she moaned.

Liothel took a deep, smoky breath, and leaped into Christine's mind.

Instantly she stood on the same black plain as before, under the same gray sky; and at once the soulworm loomed over her in dragon form, dripping jaws reaching to tear her apart, eyes burning red with hatred. But this time Liothel expected the attack, and armed her dream-self with lance and sword and prancing horse—all of which proved useless as the dragon opened its mouth and spewed flame.

Liothel tried to create a shield on her arm, but was a fraction too late; fire seared her, no less agonizing for being illusory, and she fell from the blackened carcass of her horse. A huge clawed foot swept down to pluck her from the plain—

—but she wasn't there. Massive, immovable, she had become rock, an upthrust spire of granite. The plain rang with the soulworm's evil laughter, the fear it had displayed scant seconds before swallowed once again in its spawning frenzy. "To drive me into your cursed Circle, you must first drive me from this place. Instead you cower. I have nothing to fear from you! You will burn in your own fire, while my followers will be here in seconds to rescue me. Tonight you die, and tonight I spawn, and tomorrow this world will be mine!" With that, the soulworm became a giant, wielding a steel hammer, which it raised over its head and brought down on Liothel-rock with a ringing crash.

Pain exploded in her. She concentrated on hardness, density, imperviousness, but she knew she couldn't last. She had to change again, somehow put the soulworm on the run, drive it away, but she couldn't think, the pain was too much, the pain...

Dimly she felt the floor beneath her knees, and realized she knelt at Christine's feet, arms wrapped around her head, grovelling, while Christine laughed and the flames leaped higher and higher around them, raining chunks of red-hot plaster from the ceiling, searing their lungs with scorching air and thick gray smoke. They couldn't survive much longer, and the thought came to her that if she could not defeat the soulworm on the dark plain, where hammer-blows still thundered on her crumbling dream-image, she would have to use the last of her fading strength to drive Christine into the flames, burn her alive—

—and Maribeth—

She raised tear-filled eyes. Adam was gone, must have fled through the door soon after she lit the fire. For a moment she despaired, thinking he had deserted her after all; but above the crackle and pop of the fire she heard shouting and the sound of breaking wood, and she thrust despair away again. He was out there trying to hold off the Ice Devils, buying her time. "Your Devils aren't coming," Liothel whispered hoarsely. "You'll die here before they get past Adam."

But then a single, horrible noise split the raging air—the crack of a gunshot, a flat, evil sound that made Liothel's ears ring. Christine laughed, throwing her head back, almost howling. "It begins!"

"Adam," Liothel breathed, then, "Sean!" she screamed, as a small, half-naked boy-shaped rocket burst into the room through the still-open window, through the flames that wreathed it, and careened into Christine, sending her staggering back.

"Leave her alone!"

"Sean, no!" Liothel cried, but already Christine had seized him, though he kicked and struggled and tried to bite her.

And then Christine laughed again, both on the shadowy plain and in firelit reality. "Delicious! A bridge over the fire. I'll burn your little brother alive and walk out over his body."

"You couldn't—" Smoke had scraped Liothel's throat raw.

"Watch me." Christine took one step toward the doorway, clutching Sean, his bare skin already turning red with the heat, his thin body writhing—

—and something stirred in Liothel, something deep and hidden. The scene around her whirled and receded. Someone else was in her body, someone else...Maribeth! Liothel realized in horror. No! Not now—

There was no time left. Liothel rushed fully onto the dark plain again, into the soulworm's mind, forcing it to meet her there. Liothel's stone erupted upward, became a living statue as big as the soulworm's giant. She swung a massive fist of rock, driving the soulworm back. She took a step forward and swung again, and again the other giant staggered. But then it stiffened, changed, became a glittering snake of steel that twined around Liothel's stone legs and began crushing—

An image swirled up out of nowhere, not into the dream-battle, but into Liothel/Maribeth's shared mind. Maribeth lay hurting, unable to move, watching orange flame erupt beneath the car. Christine stood, dazed but not seriously injured, on the other side. The driver's door had been ripped off; Tom, crumpled in his seat, trapped by the steering wheel, moaned and tossed his head. All Christine had to do was take six steps, grab his arms and pull him out—and she didn't. Instead she just stood rooted to the ground, staring at the car, staring at Tom, until the flames suddenly took fiercer hold and rushed around him, and Tom screamed—

The image exploded in Liothel's mind, upward and outward, sweeping into the dream scene, overpowering it. No longer a giant, Liothel was Maribeth, lying there, and the soulworm was Christine, and Tom, trapped in the front seat, looked like Sean, and again the car caught fire, only this time it was Sean's shrill scream that ripped through the night—

And abruptly there was a fourth presence, a presence Liothel had not felt before, superimposed on the soulworm. The Christine-image wavered, then split; rejoined, then split again and stayed double. And suddenly Liothel knew what she was seeing: the real Christine, the Christine that had been overpowered by the soulworm, the Christine who had been ripe for possession because of her guilt over her failure to save Tom from the fire, the horror of seeing him burn. That Christine looked at what had already happened, saw what the soulworm was about to make her do, and said, "No."

The two Christines stared at each other; then the soulworm-Christine smiled. "You haven't got the strength," it said. "You're mine—"

But Liothel and Maribeth were not split: Liothel and Maribeth were one, and although Maribeth had not fully emerged from her hiding place, still Liothel could feel her now, feel her love for Sean and for Christine-who-had-been. That love poured into her like power from one of this world's batteries, adding to her own failing strength, swelling it to proportions she could not have matched by herself even when the battle had just begun. With her Gift of Exorcism she grasped that strength and hurled it onto the dream plain.

A wall of fire a thousand feet high roared across the ebony ground, sweeping toward them with terrifying, impossible speed. The soulworm, still in Christine-form, reacting instinctively, screamed and fled before it—and vanished.

Liothel crashed through the dark plain into the inner realms of Christine's mind. The soulworm fled before her, now just a shadowy presence she could sense, twisting and turning but unable to escape, being driven to the surface not only by Liothel/Maribeth but by Christine herself, horrified at what the soulworm would have made her do. Then suddenly it was out, into the real world, surrounded by real flames. Liothel jerked her eyes open as Christine's body crumpled. "Sean, get out!" Sean hesitated. "Now!" she screamed, and he ran to the window and leaped out onto the roof below.

The soulworm, a swirl of darkness in the bloody light, flowed across the floor, dwindling, evaporating in the searing heat of the inferno that had been a room. It made a desperate lunge toward Christine, but Liothel shielded her with her mind.

Now it was down to little more than a hand's-breath in size. It darted here and there, just above the hardwood floor. For a moment the flames in the doorway subsided and it dashed toward the gap—

And Adam, appearing in that gap, brought the burning length of wood he clutched in one bloodstained hand crashing down on the soulworm. It screamed, an unheard sound that echoed in Liothel's mind, then was gone as though it had never been.

Outside, sirens sounded, barely audible above the roar of the fire. A section of the ceiling crashed down across the doorway, sending Adam staggering back, to disappear a moment later in the choking smoke. Eyes streaming, hardly able to breathe, Liothel desperately pulled Christine's limp body toward the window and forced her through it, as flames licked across the floor where they had been standing only moments before.

A ladder slammed onto the roof just below them, and a moment later a big fireman, the yellow stripes on his coat reflecting a spotlight from below, appeared over the eaves and reached out for Christine. Sean and Liothel, choking, coughing, eyes streaming sooty tears, followed under their own power, as behind them the room reached the flashover point and fire exploded through the window, showering them with hot cinders.

On the ground, Liothel ran to the nearest policeman, who was watching the last of the Ice Devils being shoved into the back of a patrol car. "There's someone else inside!" she cried through her raw throat. "Adam..."

"You called?" a hoarse voice said from behind her, and she turned to see Adam, clutching his left arm, covered with soot and blood, emerge from the smoke-shrouded front door of the farmhouse.

As Liothel and two firemen started toward him, he collapsed on the sagging porch.

28

Farewells...

A paramedic snagged Liothel before she got close to Adam; she watched, helpless, as the firemen dragged him from the porch. The paramedic fussed over her, asking her questions; the sergeant who had been at the Gayles' house stood impatiently by and asked more, but she said nothing, hardly even heard them. *Was Adam badly hurt, maybe even...*the heart she shared with Maribeth beat raggedly. To have saved this world at the expense of Adam's life...on the Creator's scales it might balance; on hers it would be unbearable.

In any event, she had made up her mind to answer no questions. There was no explanation she could give that would be taken as anything but evidence of Maribeth's mental instability. She did her best to remain mute and look like she was in shock; it wasn't hard.

Sean broke away from the paramedic tending him and ran to Liothel, seizing her in a tight hug, reeking of smoke, saying nothing, dry-eyed but shaking. Liothel ruffled his hair, feeling a tug inside as she remembered the way he had launched himself at Christine to save her...

...to save his sister. The thought hurt, and she returned Sean's hug almost fiercely. *Surely I can call him brother, too!* she told herself. *The only brother I've ever had...*

Christine really was in shock. Liothel could see it in her eyes, in the unnatural stiffness of her posture. The soulworm was gone, but the tortured girl who had proved such fertile ground for it was still there. For a moment their gazes locked, then Christine looked away. Liothel wished she could tell her everything was all right now, that what had happened in the accident wasn't her fault—but it wasn't all right, and it was her fault. She could have saved Tom. She knew it. Liothel knew it. Maribeth knew it. Christine would have to learn to live with it.

Liothel wondered if she ever could.

And then there was Maribeth. Liothel could feel her down underneath, quiescent, perhaps also in shock, in her own way, but back from wherever her horrible memories of seeing Tom die while her best friend let it happen had sent her, where she had fled again at seeing Adam in the same danger. Liothel hoped she was back for good.

Adam's stretcher was bundled through the rear doors of one ambulance; Liothel, Sean and Christine, accompanied by a big policeman, were directed into another. In its spotless white interior all three of them sat silent under the curious stare of the attendant and the impassive gaze of the cop all through the lengthy ride to the hospital high on Weyburn's only hill.

But as they emerged in front of the emergency entrance, Liothel stumbled, a wave of dizziness sweeping over her. For a moment the high walls of red brick, the glittering glass and steel and bright blue-green lights, seemed only a curious fog overlaying gray rock, ancient wood and flickering torches; then reality returned, and Liothel found the ambulance attendant holding her upright. "Let's get you inside," he said kindly. "You must have been through a lot tonight."

You don't know the half of it, Liothel thought above the pounding of her pulse, for she had instantly recognized that brief scene: Mykia.

Home.

226

But around her now were tiled floors and pale green walls. Adam had arrived first; Liothel caught a disturbing glimpse of his orange-blanketed form being wheeled down a side corridor as the rest of them were taken to separate examining rooms. A doctor came in almost at once. She let him prod her and poke her and listen to her heart and take her pulse, but she answered none of his questions, and through the narrow window of the examining room's door she saw him shaking his head as he talked to the police sergeant.

She was glad Dr. Ryback wasn't there. It would have been very hard not to answer Dr. Ryback; her shared memories with Maribeth identified the doctor as a friend. But her resolve was firm; she would talk to no one. She had already caused Maribeth untold grief. Keeping silent was her best and only way to avoid causing more.

The world reeled again; speckled tile gave way to flagstones, the swinging metal door to one of heavy black wood. Then the examining room was back, and Liothel swayed to her feet, suddenly certain that her time left in this world was down to minutes, that the Warders of Mykia knew the soulworm had been destroyed and were working to bring her home.

But she couldn't go, not yet—not without saying goodbye, to Sean, to her—Maribeth's—parents, to—

To Adam. If he was even alive. How could she leave without saying goodbye to Adam?

She pushed open the door; the doctor and sergeant were still talking just outside. The policeman who had ridden in the ambulance with them stood by, looking bored. She heard a snatch of conversation, "...fragile mental equilibrium after the coma....," and cleared her throat. The two men turned to look at her. "Where's Adam?" she asked.

The sergeant rubbed his chin. "I told the doctor you could talk, Miss Gayle. Now maybe we'll find out what this is all about."

"Not until I see Adam."

"You can't," said the doctor. "He's going into surgery as soon as Dr. Westman gets here—"

"Is he awake?"

"Yes, but—"

"Then let me see him. Only for a minute. Just long enough to—"

"To get your stories to match?" said the sergeant. "Come on, Miss Gayle. If I let you do that, I won't know if I can believe either of you."

"Then have a policeman in the room. I don't care—but unless you let me talk to him, neither one of us is going to tell you anything."

The sergeant, frowning, took a package of cigarettes from his overcoat pocket; the doctor cleared his throat and glanced pointedly at the NO SMOKING sign at the end of the hall, and the sergeant sighed and put the package back. "All right," he said. "If the doctor thinks it's safe."

"He's in no serious danger," the doctor said reluctantly. "But Dr. Westman should be here in five minutes or less—"

"Right," said the sergeant. "Five minutes. Then I want some answers." He nodded to the policeman. "You go with her."

"Yes, sir."

"Five minutes," Liothel agreed at once, propping herself against the wall with one hand as Mykia momentarily swirled around her once more.

The sergeant glanced at the doctor, who scowled, but led Liothel down the corridor to a room the twin of the one she had been examined in. He pushed open the door and let Liothel in, motioning for the nurse inside to come out.

Adam lay on a gurney, chest and arms bare, his lower body covered by a blanket. A heavy bandage, stained red, was taped to his left shoulder. Sweat-streaked soot stained the rest of his body; the sponge the nurse had been about to use to clean him up soaked in a basin on a steel table close by the gurney. His hands were red and blistered, and his face looked strangely naked, eyebrows and eyelashes and part of his hair burned away. As Liothel entered, he turned his head as though his neck hurt.

The door closed behind the nurse and opened again for the policeman, who stood just inside it, watching them. Liothel ignored him. "How—how are you?" she said to Adam, her voice trembling a little.

"I've been better," Adam whispered. He coughed once, and winced.

"They shot you—"

"Yeah, well, I was lucky they didn't think of it before. They seemed confused, like they didn't know what they were doing there—and they saw the police coming up the drive. If they'd been as organized as they were when they attacked your house..."

"The soulworm had too many things to do at once. The links it had built with the Ice Devils gave way...but I didn't come here to talk about this." She glanced at the policeman. They might have been in another city for all the reaction he showed, but Liothel had no doubt he was mentally noting everything they said to each other, and wondered what he would think of it. She pulled a chair from the wall and sat down beside Adam. "I came to say goodbye."

Adam blinked. "Goodbye?"

"This is where the Gate is. I can feel the Warders calling me back. It's getting—" The world blinked out, then on again. "It's getting stronger all the time," she said breathlessly, clutching the edge of the gurney.

Adam closed his eyes. "Maybe it's a good thing," he murmured. "I don't think I could survive having you around much longer."

Liothel was shocked by hot tears suddenly flooding her eyes. "I'm...sorry..." she choked out. "It's all been—I didn't know what else to do—"

"Oh, Mari—Liothel!" Adam's eyes fluttered open again and his right hand found hers. "I'm sorry, I didn't mean it the way it sounded. It's just—" He managed a weak smile. "It's been kind of a rough night."

Liothel linked fingers with him. "It has, hasn't it?"

There was a moment of silence. Adam's hand tightened. "You're really leaving?"

"I think so."

"What do I tell—" He flicked his eyes toward the silent cop.

"Tell them the truth—as much as they'll believe—about the Ice Devils, and Sean." She dropped her voice to a bare whisper. "Just don't tell them you were saving the world from a demon from another dimension."

Adam grinned. "I won't." His smile died quickly, though. "I'm going to miss you."

Liothel felt a lump in her throat, tried to swallow it and couldn't. "I'm going to miss you, too," she said in a small voice. Her future as a Warder loomed in her mind—the goal she had thought she would never achieve. No one could say now she wasn't worthy. She had proved it to everyone, even to herself. But—never to know the sweetness of a kiss again, the warmth of an embrace, love...she shook her head. "At least you'll still have Maribeth." It came out sharper than she intended. "I can feel her inside—she's coming back."

His hand tightened on hers again, and his eyes brightened. "She's not you," he said.

But involuntary reaction had told Liothel the truth, and both sadness and relief filled her: sadness that, despite the warmth of Adam's affection, he didn't truly love her—how could he, when he had never known her complete, whole, in her own body?—but relief that she had not destroyed every good thing in Maribeth's life. Adam might not love Maribeth, either—not really. But Liothel thought he would learn to. And as for Maribeth...

"No," she said. "She's not me. But—she likes you, you know. A lot."

Adam's face lit up. "You—you know that?"

"I have her memories." For a moment longer Liothel held Adam's hand, then let go. "And she has mine," she added huskily. "She'll remember—the time she was gone."

Adam looked a little alarmed. "What will she—you know—think?"

But Liothel was unable to answer. The room was receding from her, whirling away and fading. "I'm leaving now!" she cried, but heard no sound.

I'm not ready! she protested to emptiness. *I didn't say goodbye to Sean, or Maribeth's parents, or Crystal and Ellen, or...*

"They've never known you were here," a gentler voice, someone else's voice, whispered inside her. *"How can you say goodbye?"*

"Jara?"

"Come home, little one." The Warder's voice tugged at her like a cord, the pull growing stronger and stronger. *"Come home..."*

But something still held Liothel back, though she could see the Gate in her mind now, glowing like the promise of the sun in the final minutes before dawn. For a moment she turned away from it, looked out across the shadowy plain where she had fought the soulworm—and saw the one she wanted to say goodbye to most of all, standing by the burned-out wreckage of a car.

"Maribeth?"

"This is very strange. Am I dreaming?"

"In a way."

"All this stuff I remember...fires and kidnappings and guns...is it real?"

"Yes. I'm afraid I've left you quite a mess."

Maribeth looked at the wreck. *"This was what I was afraid to remember, isn't it? Tom burning, and Christine just standing there...how could she do that?"*

"She was afraid."

"I always thought she was so brave..."

"She is. She helped me drive out the soulworm. She's coming back."

"But how can it ever be the same between us?"

Liothel said nothing. *It can't,* she thought. *But at least you once had a best friend. And now you have a boy who will love you, and a brother who would risk his life for you, and parents who worry about you...*

"Maybe it will be better," she said at last. "Maribeth, you have to wake up now. Your parents are on their way. Adam is about to go into surgery. He's waiting for you. So is Sean." She paused. "And Christine."

"My parents...they think I've turned against them. They'll think I don't love them any more—and the house, our home—what have you done to me? What have you done to us?" Her "voice" grew louder, angrier. "How dare you come in here—inside me—and—"

For a moment Liothel cringed from her anger, from the questions she herself had asked so often, but then something new seemed to stand up inside her, to calm her and strengthen her. "Maribeth, remember the soulworm. Use the memories we have shared these last few days. You will keep them, as I will. Whatever pain I have caused you, I'm sorry for, more than you know—but remember the soulworm, what it did to Christine, what it would have done to Sean, to Adam, to everyone—and know that it was worth it."

Maribeth stood silent. *I know it was,* she said at last. *"But it's going to be hard for a while to believe that...though someday I may thank you for some of the things you've shown me about my family and friends—and Adam."* She smiled suddenly, and a weight Liothel hadn't know was there seemed to vanish from her heart. *"But right now, Liothel, there's only one thing that really concerns me— how am I going to explain all this?"*

Liothel grinned at her. "Don't try. Just tell them you haven't been yourself recently."

Maribeth gaped, and then suddenly laughed, and on the wings of that laughter vanished, riding mirth like a cleansing breeze into the misty sky above the dark plain, into the world and the future that were hers, leaving behind the burned-out hulk of the car, a memory made visible, a boil lanced. Liothel listened to the echoes of Maribeth's laughter, and when it faded, knew that Maribeth was back in her own body, Adam by her side, her parents on their way, her brother nearby, her best friend starting a long road back—and her world safe from the evil spawned in Liothel's.

It should have been a happy ending, but as Liothel turned back toward the Gate and plunged through it, she thought she felt, fleeting as a feather's touch, Adam's lips upon her own.

29

...And New Beginnings

Maribeth left Adam as Dr. Westman entered the examining room. The sergeant turned toward her, but Maribeth had eyes only for the room across the hall, from which Christine was emerging.

The two girls looked at each other; then Christine said, softly, "Maribeth? Is that you?"

"Christine?"

A smile flickered across Christine's face, then was gone; but for the moment, thought Maribeth, it was enough.

Her parents entered the far end of the corridor. An instant later she was enveloped in their arms; and though she knew many bridges between them would yet have to be rebuilt, for the moment, that, too, was enough.

Goodbye, Liothel, she thought, and snuggled closer in her parents' embrace.

ɞ ɞ ɞ ɞ ɞ

"There's nothing I can say to make you change your mind, is there?" Jara said, watching Liothel tighten the girth of the saddle.

"Jara, you've already used every argument twice. I'm going!" Liothel gave the strap a final tug and then stepped back to examine everything one last time. All her supplies, enough for two weeks on the road, were tightly bound in place, and the horse was a fine beast; it turned and met her appraising look with one of its own, making her chuckle.

"We're going to miss you," Jara said. *"I'm* going to miss you. You know you've always been special to me. And Kalia—"

"Jara, you're the dearest person in the world to me, you know that. But we've been through all this." She turned and smiled affectionately at the older woman. "I was stuck in bed for a week after I came back. I had a lot of time to think about my life—who I am, where I came from, what I really want to do and be. And I realized I couldn't be a Warder until I had something to ward. Family, friends—something." She gestured around at the courtyard, surrounded by stables, just off the main gate of Mykia. "Look at this place, Jara. Stone walls, stone streets—a garden or two up top—a forest all around. This is all the world I've ever known. But that doesn't mean it's all the world. And now..."

"Now you've lived another's life," Jara said quietly. "Liothel, was it really that much better than yours?"

"Don't you understand, Jara? She wasn't alone."

"The Warders are your family..."

"It's not the same." She climbed up into the saddle, and the horse moved restlessly under her, eager to be off. "As for Kalia—Jara, she doesn't remember me. She doesn't remember anything that happened from the time the soulworm took her. But I remember. And remembering what I do—I don't think she needs me around." She took up the reins. "I've been planning this for three months, Jara. You won't talk me out of it now."

"Are you sure this isn't just castle fever? Do you really know what you're looking for?"

Liothel nodded. "Yes, Jara. I do." *A brother like Sean,* she thought. *Parents like Maribeth's. A friend like*

Christine used to be...someone to hold me, like Adam. "And maybe it's not out there—but maybe it is. I have to look."

Jara smiled a little. "I suppose you do. And Prisca knows you've more than done your duty as a Warder." She released the bridle. "May the Creator smile on your journey. And may He bring you back to us one day."

Liothel looked up the hill, at the Keep shining white in the morning sun. Just like Maribeth had taken refuge in a coma, so she had taken refuge behind those thick stone walls, refuge in her role as perpetual, aging Acolyte, refuge in her self-doubt: if she were unable to do anything worthwhile, then no one would ever expect her to do anything at all. But she was not an Acolyte any longer, and she had succeeded at a great task—those spiritual refuges were gone. Now it was time to leave her physical refuge, too; time to face the world, to take the risk of finding out if she were all alone on the chance that she was not. And even if she had no family, still there could be companions, friends...

...someone like Adam...

Liothel clucked to the horse, and rode out of Wardfast Mykia, over the clattering drawbridge and into the forest, aglow with spring's first delicate green. She had explored a world and a life strange beyond imagining; it was time to explore her own.

THE END